MEET ME
IN THE PARK,
ANGIE

WESTMINSTER PRESS BOOKS BY
PHYLLIS ANDERSON WOOD

Meet Me in the Park, Angie

HIWAY

Pass Me a Pine Cone
This Time Count Me In
Get a Little Lost, Tia
Win Me and You Lose
I Think This Is Where We Came In
A Five-Color Buick and a Blue-Eyed Cat
Song of the Shaggy Canary

MEET ME
IN THE PARK,
ANGIE

Phyllis Anderson Wood

*To The students
of Sacred Heart School*

Best wishes

Phyllis Wood

May 1992

THE WESTMINSTER PRESS
Philadelphia

F
WOD

Book Design by Alice Derr

First edition

Published by The Westminster Press®
Philadelphia, Pennsylvania

PRINTED IN THE UNITED STATES OF AMERICA
9   8   7   6   5   4   3   2   1

Library of Congress Cataloging in Publication Data

Wood, Phyllis Anderson.
   Meet me in the park, Angie.

   SUMMARY: Teenage newlyweds, he a city gardener, she a waitress, struggle through problems of unemployment, jealousy, threats against a pet, and adjustment to each other.
   [1. Marriage—Fiction] I. Title.
PZ7.W854Me 1983   [Fic]   83–16937
ISBN 0–664–32710–9

11237

To Roger

who has been
a perfect publishing partner

ONE

As Peter Ohlinger moved in his sleep, the gold wedding band on his left hand caught an early-morning sunbeam. A tiny reflection danced crazily across the bedroom wall.

Angie Ohlinger, already awake, lay beside her husband, lost in thought. Slowly she moved her hand around in the sunlight until her own wedding ring caught a golden beam, too. Angie smiled and made her ring's reflection chase Peter's around the room.

It still doesn't seem real, Angie thought, even after six months. Me married to Peter Ohlinger. He's so grown-up at nineteen, and look at me. Would anyone believe I'm eighteen and married?

Anyway, I know for sure Peter loves me, Angie marveled, and I love him. With a comfortable sigh, she stretched out full length and wiggled her toes.

The sun hit Peter's face. He turned away from the light and opened his eyes. Angie's eyes were inches away. Peter grinned and pulled her to him.

"Forget it," Angie warned, drawing away from Peter's kiss. "I have to be at work in forty minutes, and so do you." She jumped out of bed, grabbed her blue-

and-white Ranch Burger uniform, and headed for the shower.

"Aw, come on back to bed, Angie," Peter pleaded. "You won't even miss a few minutes."

"Maybe I wouldn't," Angie called back, "but my boss sure would."

Peter got up, stretched, and leaned against the wall by the bathroom door, yawning.

"Hey," he shouted above the splashing water, "if I don't get into that shower soon, I'll lose an hour's pay."

"I'm out, I'm out," Angie sang as she stepped from the shower. She slid past Peter's outstretched arms. His eyes followed her.

The look on her husband's face made Angie worry that she had hurt his feelings. She blew him a kiss.

"Give me a raincheck on the invitation, okay?" she murmured.

"No rainchecks, lady." Peter's face was deadpan. "You miss a game, too bad."

He stepped into the shower, leaving Angie wondering if maybe she should have gone back for a little more time with him. She didn't always know how to take his teasing.

As the water poured over him, Peter put together his workday in his mind: finish planting the traffic island at Mission and Cypress, replace six trees on Citrus Avenue, repair the motorcycle tracks in the City Hall lawn. Not a bad day, he decided, unless the foreman teams me up with Manny.

Peter frowned as he thought of his fellow worker on the city gardeners crew. Wonder how that guy ever slipped through? I didn't know awful people went into gardening.

Smelling of herbal aftershave, Peter drifted into the

tiny kitchen. Angie passed a hand across his smooth shirt as he started setting out some eggs and a frypan.

"Mmm, you've got to be the nicest-smelling gardener in the city."

"Thank you, ma'am," Peter drawled. "This fragrance is called Morning Manure, for the masterful male. Sensuous, yet earthy."

Angie glanced at her husband and grinned. "Thanks a lot." She stepped back, holding her nose. "Here. The coffee's all made. I've got to run."

As she passed, Peter caught the skirt of Angie's Ranch Burger uniform. "Doesn't the waitress pour coffee for the customers in this coffee shop?" He tugged teasingly.

"For my customers, I pour coffee. But then, of course, I never date a customer." Angie smiled at her logic.

"You got me," Peter admitted, serving himself. "And now about that date with the waitress."

"Later," Angie said over her shoulder. She sailed out the door.

Peter rushed to the doorway. "Want me to pick you up on my way home?"

"I'm not sure what time I'll get off," Angie called back. "Meet you here, instead. Bye."

Within minutes, Peter was ready to leave, too. He locked the apartment door and stepped back to study the entrance.

On payday, he thought, on payday I'm going to buy a redwood tub and a *Pseudosasa japonica*—to go right there. He measured the angle with his hands.

Yeah, on payday—famous last words.

Peter was studying his front door again nine hours later, when Angie arrived home.

"Hi," he said. "I could have picked you up after all."

"It's okay. I really expected to have a short shift today."

Peter unlocked the door, letting Angie slip by him. She held an open paper bag in her arms, one hand under it.

"Did you go to the market?"

Angie shook her head.

"That's why you have a shopping bag, because you didn't shop."

Angie nodded.

"Let me guess. They gave you a dozen Ranch Burgers for our dinner."

Angie held her stomach. "Please, not that!"

Setting the bag gently on the table, Angie reached in and lifted out a tiny gray kitten. As she held it to her cheek, it began to meow.

Peter stared at the furry ball. "What is that?"

"That is a cat." Angie tried to act casual. She already expected Peter's next reaction.

"And what does our lease say about having pets in this apartment?"

"It says no." Angie stroked the kitten frantically as she spoke. "Remember how thick the fog was this morning? Well, during the night someone left three kittens in a box in the Ranch Burger parking lot. When I got there, this one was wandering around in the fog, crying."

Peter started to speak, but Angie hurried on with her nervous explanation. "I named her Fog. Because she was lost in it. See? Don't you like the name?"

"Angie, you're explaining the wrong things. The name is cute. The kitten is cute. But . . . the lease says no pets. If we keep her, the landlord will throw us out.

There are no other apartments at this price."

"Maybe we could just try it?" Angie suggested wistfully. "Look, Peter." She pulled a box of kitten food from the bag. "The people who abandoned the kittens left three boxes of kitty food with them."

"She's probably hungry right now," Peter said, opening the box and mixing some food. "She'd better eat while we decide what to do with her."

Peter set the bowl of food on the floor, and Angie put Fog near it. They watched, fascinated, while the tiny kitten took delicate bites from the dish.

"We can't afford to lose this apartment," Peter said slowly, his resistance beginning to crumble.

"Who's going to know—"

A knock on the door stopped Angie in midsentence. She scooped up Fog and the dish of food and scurried into the bathroom. Peter shoved the box of kitten chow into the cupboard before answering the door.

It turned out to be the news carrier, collecting for the month's papers. Peter paid him, let out a relieved sigh, and closed the door quickly.

"The fugitive can come out of hiding," he called.

Angie brought Fog and the food dish out of the bathroom and set them both on the carpet near Peter.

"Tell me you don't think Fog's adorable, Peter. Go on. Try to say it. I dare you."

"We agree—she's adorable. And so is our cheap apartment."

Angie hugged the purring kitten. "What harm can she do anyone? She doesn't bark. She'll use a litter pan. Who's she going to bother?"

"The landlord, I'm afraid. Mr. Rottweiler, the guy who makes leases. That's who."

Angie put the kitten on the floor and went to the

window, standing with her back to Peter. After staring out for a long time, she finally said, "If we aren't going to have a baby for a while, don't you think we need something little to love? Something soft and cuddly?"

"How about you?" Peter suggested. "You're soft and cuddly."

Angie didn't react to his comment. She continued to gaze into the distance.

Peter picked up the kitten, studied her thoughtfully, and then set her on the floor again.

"What happens," he asked, "if we make a cat a member of the family, and then the landlord orders us to get rid of her?"

Angie snapped to life. "He won't," she promised, whirling around. "She'll be good. I'll see to it. And we'll be supercareful about the landlord." She picked up the kitten again and held her close.

"It sounds risky. Crazy. Against my better judgment," Peter said, almost to himself.

"Mine, too," Angie whispered. "But she's worth it. Here, want to hug her?" Angie held the kitten out to Peter.

"That's okay." Peter backed away, still not ready to surrender.

"We won't be sorry," Angie said.

"We probably will," Peter contradicted. "I don't want to be around the day you're told to get rid of your cat."

Angie overlooked Peter's final doubts. "You know what? I married a big softy."

"Yeah. Just a marshmallow inside." Peter held out his arms. "Want to hug a marshmallow?"

"Anytime." Angie set the cat down and went to Peter.

Keeping one arm around Angie, Peter leaned down and picked up Fog. Holding the kitten close to his face, he studied the furry features.

"What have I done?" he murmured. "I think I've just adopted you." Peter shook his head slowly. "I don't believe it, Angie. Have I just become Fog's father?"

Angie backed off and looked critically at the big man and the tiny cat.

"There is a family resemblance," she told him. "Especially around the eyes."

"Meow," Peter agreed.

The new family crumpled in a laughing heap on the couch. Fog fought her way to the surface and draped herself across Peter's knee, purring.

Being careful not to disturb the kitten, Peter reached for the television remote control and turned on the news. For half an hour he sat with an arm around Angie and a hand on Fog, savoring his role as a family man.

The news ended and Peter turned off the television.

"Hungry?" Angie asked.

Peter pulled her closer.

"No, stay here," he said softly. "This is nice. You don't have to break it up to play housewife."

Angie snuggled closer. Peter tightened his hold on her.

"Forget the world," he murmured. "Forget our jobs. Forget our budget. Forget everything."

"Just you and me," Angie sighed. "Together forever —like they say on the valentines."

"Peter and Angela Ohlinger." Peter was testing the ring of it. "Sounds solid," he decided. "A little hard to say, maybe, with the Angela next to the O."

Angie smiled. "Now that we're friends, why don't you just call me Angie?"

"Lady, we're way beyond friends," Peter said. "By now we should at least be down to Anj."

"I'll go for the Ohlingers," Angie decided. "I like the sound of it. The Ohlingers—Peter and Angie."

An insistent meowing broke the spell.

"Oops," Angie said. "Don't forget Fog."

"Fog Ohlinger." Peter picked up the cat to test the name. "Fog Ohlinger? Honey, couldn't you have found a fancier name than Fog?"

"Hey, come on," Angie protested. "Don't you even know Carl Sandburg's poem that says 'Fog comes on little cat feet'?"

"Say, that's good!" Peter exclaimed. "That's very good." He turned to the cat. "See? The lady's not so dumb."

Peter flashed Angie a teasing look. Then he turned back to the kitten in his hand. "And she can cook, too."

In response to the hint, Angie pulled herself to her feet.

"You going to help fix dinner," she asked, "or are you going to be a big, fat chauvinist and let the little woman do it?"

"What do you mean, a chauvinist? I'm going to do some parenting while you cook."

Peter stretched out on the couch and draped Fog across his stomach. The kitten melted into relaxed sleep, purring as Peter rubbed her chin.

"I don't suppose you could take time out from your father act to eat, could you?" Angie asked later, as she set two dinners on the table.

Peter hobbled over to the table with Fog on his lap. "Looks great, honey." He settled into the chair without the cat's ever waking up. "This sure beats those Ranch Burgers I thought you had in the bag."

14

"Anything could beat them," Angie replied. "But Ranch Burgers are better than Ranch Wiches. They are truly the worst."

"How does that place keep its customers?" Peter asked.

"They don't. No one ever comes back. It's all highway trade—and that's dropping off."

Peter's expression turned serious. "Do you think they'll go out of business?"

"Probably."

"Have they mentioned laying you off?"

"That's coming."

Peter turned to his plate. He picked at his food, lost in thought.

"Do you care?" he asked, breaking the silence.

"About what?"

"About losing the Ranch Burger job?"

"Well, it's money. With no training, I probably can't get anything much better."

"Want to get into one of the programs at Crestline College? Learn a trade?"

"Come on. You know how I hated school, Peter. Remember, you wrote my last paper to get me through English so I could graduate?"

Peter laughed at the memory.

"You're the one who should go to college," Angie said. "Not me. You should be a landscape designer instead of a city gardener."

For a long time Peter chased the same three peas around his plate with a fork, seeming not to care that the peas were winning.

"I can't go to college," he mumbled. "We couldn't possibly get along if I had only a part-time job." He lapsed into silence again, staring absently at the fork in his hand.

After a moment, Peter stood up. He set Fog on Angie's lap, walked into the bedroom, and quietly closed the door.

Angie held the warm kitten to her cheek and stared at the closed door.

TWO

For a long time Angie sat at the table, lost in thought. While her hand mechanically stroked Fog, her mind darted around.

This was a side of Peter she had never seen—a curtain of silence, shutting her out, and just at the moment when they had become a little family.

What did I say? Angie tried to retrace the conversation. Was I cutting down his job? I thought he was glad to have a permanent job with the city. Maybe the money. That's it. Now I remember, he was worrying about my being laid off. Her thoughts were so jumbled that she gave up. If only he'd talk . . .

Angie set Fog on the floor and cleared the table like a kitchen robot. She had to stand very still while she washed dishes at the sink, because Fog lay down on her left foot.

Although Angie kept glancing toward the door, hoping Peter would open it, nothing but silence came from the bedroom.

When the dishes were done, Angie prepared for Fog's first night. She put a bath towel in a box, fixed bowls of food and water, and spread out some newspapers nearby.

"Now, little girl," she told the cat, "I have other things to deal with. You be good." Amazed, Angie watched the kitten curl up happily in the box and go to sleep.

With her hand on the bedroom doorknob, Angie paused to listen for sounds inside. She turned the knob, relieved that at least she wasn't locked out.

Although twilight had given way to darkness, Angie could see that Peter was lying on the bed, staring at the ceiling.

Not sure what to do, Angie sat down on the bed and put a hand on Peter's arm. If she touched him, he would surely reach out and pull her close, the way he always did.

"Honey," she said softly. "Don't shut me out. Talk to me. Did I do something, say something?"

Peter reached for the comforter at the foot of the bed and pulled it over him. He turned on his side, facing the wall.

Angie's shoulders sagged. She sat for a moment, biting her lip. What next? she wondered. You can't lie beside someone who's put up a wall.

She shivered nervously. Has he gone to sleep for the night? Where should I go?

Finally she took her own pillow and went to the couch. She turned the stereo on softly, tucked her feet under her, and huddled under the hand-knitted throw blanket which had been a wedding gift from Aunt Dorothy.

The tears began—a single one at first. Angie wiped it away with her hand. Then more—Angie dried them on the pillowcase. Finally a torrent—Angie buried her

18

face in the pillow and sobbed until she had no tears left.

The moment she pulled Aunt Dorothy's afghan up to her face, a flood of memories washed over Angie. The wedding gifts . . . the loving wishes . . . little joking warnings . . . and through it all, Peter. The one who could deal with everything. So responsible, everyone said.

Angie tightened her grip on the afghan. She rubbed it against her cheek, noticing for the first time the tension in her jaw.

Feeling the urge to try again, Angie tiptoed into the bedroom. Once again, she sat on the edge of the bed, hoping to be pulled close.

Maybe my bringing home a cat was too much. One more responsibility, one more reminder that at age nineteen his freedom is already gone?

Should I give up Fog? she wondered. Quickly, Angie knew she didn't feel that sorry. No, definitely no!

Maybe he wishes we hadn't gotten married. Angie clutched the blanket against the chilling thought.

Peter's steady breathing told Angie that her plan to talk was wishful thinking. He was gone for the night.

With the afghan trailing behind like a security blanket, Angie went back to the couch and wrapped herself miserably in her wedding gift.

For a while Angie dozed fitfully, waking often to listen for sounds from Peter. Finally she slept, turning uncomfortably on the couch, trying to find some way to fit on it.

When Angie awakened, the morning sunshine was filtering through the drapes. She opened her eyes slowly. Her neck hurt. Her knees were cramped. Her head ached.

Angie's concern for Peter's private suffering shifted to her own misery. Standing up stiffly, she tried to get the kink out of her back.

That bed's half mine, she thought resentfully. I've been working to help pay for it. She rubbed her back as she hobbled toward the bedroom. And I have to sleep on the couch? That's crazy. Now she was truly sorry for herself.

Grabbing some clean clothes from the dresser drawer, Angie slammed the drawer hard. She stomped noisily into the bathroom, making a ceremony of locking the door. Only then did she realize that the bed had been empty.

Nursing her resentment as the shower poured over her, Angie didn't even wonder where Peter was.

Dressed, she stalked into the living room, planning not to talk to Peter. If he wouldn't talk last night, why should she talk this morning?

When Angie picked up the afghan to fold it, she found the bedroom comforter along with it. The last time she had seen that comforter, it was wrapping the silent giant like a mummy. Angie chose not to think about how or why it had covered her as she slept.

Peter was gone. His breakfast dishes were washed and put neatly in the drainer.

A note on the table said, "Angie, why didn't you come to bed?" Angie covered the writing with the sugar bowl.

Pausing from drawer-slamming and stomping around, Angie looked over at Fog's box. The food and water bowls were freshly filled. Fog was contentedly playing with a tennis ball.

Angie gulped down some breakfast, standing at the sink, because she didn't want to sit near Peter's note.

She brushed her teeth, again making a useless dramatic gesture of locking the bathroom. Then she grabbed her jacket and started out the front door.

Angie paused at the threshold, then went back to pat Fog's head. On a sudden impulse, she went to the table and stared for a moment at the sugar bowl. Finally, she lifted it off the note and scrawled in big letters, "BECAUSE *YOU* FROZE ME OUT!!!"

That settled, she left for work.

Angie punished the sidewalk. Her feet pounded as she hurried toward the Ranch Burger. She punished the hand-operated signal light at the crossing, jabbing at it until it finally surrendered. She punished the back door of the coffee shop. Then, seeing the manager's frown, she apologized.

"Sorry, Mr. Ryan. The wind caught it."

The day went down from there. Angie spilled a glass of ice water, and it drenched her right shoe. She burned three burgers while tending the French fries. Somehow she made wrong change and came out five dollars short at the noon counting.

When Angie finally plopped down at lunchtime with a Ranch Burger and a glass of milk, she was near tears. That was the moment Mr. Ryan chose to move in for the kill. He sat down at her table, looking across at her.

"Angie, I'm going to have to lay you off."

Angie barely heard his explanation. In panic, she began to add up their household expenses.

"Business is so bad," Mr. Ryan continued, "that I can't even afford a countergirl. I'm going to have to work it myself." He tapped Angie's arm. "Did you hear?"

Angie nodded. "When's my last day?"

"Today."

Leaving her Ranch Burger half eaten, Angie got up and went into the rest room. She stared in disgust at the distorted reflection in the cheap mirror. You're a mess, she decided. You're supposed to have a few things together by the time you're eighteen—especially if you're married. Look at you!

Angie dragged through the afternoon, watching the clock and worrying.

At five o'clock, with her final paycheck in her pocket, she walked home. As she mentally tried out different ways of breaking the news to Peter, she completely forgot that she wasn't even speaking to him.

Angie approached the apartment door, her eyes on the ground and her mind on her problem. She pulled out her key, then backed off. Oops, wrong door.

She looked again. Nope—right door, new look. Angie stood off to get a better view of the bamboo clump in the redwood tub, now marking the Ohlinger apartment.

Very classy, Angie decided. Peter knows just what to do with a plant.

Wonder what he does with dumb wives who lose jobs, though. She took a deep breath, quietly unlocked the door, and peeked in.

Peter was at the sink, washing vegetables. Fog was batting the tennis ball around his feet.

Angie closed the front door softly and tiptoed to the couch. Since the water was running, Peter hadn't heard her. He moved around the kitchen, tripping over the kitten several times. Finally, he picked Fog up and put her in her box. "Now," he told the kitten, "you play in your playpen while I get dinner. It's safer that way."

Angie cleared her throat nervously. Surprised, Peter turned toward the living room. Angie gave him a weak little wave, not knowing what to do next.

Peter dried his hands and came into the living room. "Like the *Pseudosasa japonica* in the tub by the door?"

"Love it!"

"I hoped you would."

"It must have cost a lot."

"I figured we could handle it this month. Your paycheck has really helped, Angie."

Angie's stomach did a double flip.

"Used to help." She pulled her paycheck from her pocket and waved it uneasily. "My last. I got laid off."

Peter looked stunned.

"Go on. Yell at me," Angie pleaded. "Get mad . . . scream . . . do something."

"I wasn't brought up to yell and scream about problems," Peter answered.

Angie didn't hear. "Tell me I'm a handicap to you. I cost more than I'm worth." Her voice was rising. "I'm immature . . . shouldn't be married . . . can't handle the responsibility." She rushed on, hysterically. "Tell me that, Peter. Go on and yell at me, will you? Yell . . . yell . . . just don't go silent on me again!"

That comment brought a troubled look to Peter's face.

Angie's high-pitched voice became shrill. "Don't go away again."

Peter rushed to take her in his arms. "Shh, shh." He pressed her head to his chest.

"You never should have married me."

"Shh." Peter's big hand covered the side of Angie's head. He patted her gently until she began to sob softly.

Peter pulled Angie over to the couch, stroking her hair until her sobbing stopped. He wiped her cheeks with his hands. She wiped his shirtfront where her tears had left streaks.

"All right," Peter said quietly, "tell me what this is all about."

"I told you. I lost my job."

"That job isn't worth a big scene. It was a crummy burger stand, anyway."

Peter pulled Angie around so he could look her in the eye. "Now," he said firmly, "what's this really about? What's this talk of my going away again?"

"Like when you put up the wall last night." Angie's explanation seemed lame.

"What wall?"

Peter stood up and walked over to the window, leaving Angie biting her fingernail on the couch. He stared out, his back to the room.

"You're starting it again," Angie said, her voice rising nervously. "It's when you quit talking. You go away. I can't get near you. Don't you love me?"

"What a dumb question."

"Now you're calling me dumb!"

"I'm *not* calling you dumb. It's simply a dumb question."

"I know I'm not the smartest wife in the world, but—"

"Will you quit talking like that!"

"I just know that I'm smart enough to share your problems. To talk about things with you. And when you shut me out—"

Peter turned from the window and walked into the bedroom. Angie sagged on the couch. Here we go again, she thought.

After a moment, Angie walked to the bedroom door. Peter was sitting on the bed.

"Don't do it again tonight," she begged softly.

Peter looked up, his face troubled. "Do what?"

"Don't shut me out," she pleaded.

Silently, Peter opened his arms to Angie. She went to him, wanting him to hold her tenderly.

Peter's embrace was strong. He pulled her down onto the bed with him. Angie rolled away.

"No," she said. "Don't make love to me."

"Angie," Peter pleaded.

"No!" she replied flatly. "Talk to me, Peter. Just talk to me."

Peter lay there, studying his wife.

"I married you," Angie said wistfully. "Remember? I promised to share my life with you. Well, how can I share anything if you won't talk?"

Angie set her terms. "Talk first! Okay?"

Peter nodded and opened his arms. Angie rolled back in.

"Honey, there are some things I don't even know how to talk about." Peter's explanation was uncertain. "Like feelings. I don't know how to share them with someone. I never have."

"Start with last night," Angie urged, "when you left the table and went to bed. How did you feel?"

There was a long silence. Angie could feel Peter's heartbeat. Finally he spoke, haltingly.

"Tender. I felt very tender. So much so that it almost hurt. I loved you. I loved the way Fog made us feel like a family. I wanted us to be a family. And then you mentioned school. And I want to go to school, too. The trouble is, I want everything. I want it all too soon. I don't know how to give up a dream."

Peter took a long, deep breath. It came out as a sigh.

"So, why should you give up the dream?" Angie

25

asked. She kissed Peter tenderly. "Can't we work on it together?"

Peter returned the kiss, tenderly at first, then urgently. Now his wife was a willing lover—no more talking.

THREE

FOR a while, Angie and Peter lay on the bed, feeling close without words. Finally Peter spoke.

"It's scary. You know that?"

"What's scary?"

"The way people can interpret things wrong. Like you thinking I didn't love you, and me being so overwhelmed with feelings that I couldn't even deal with them."

"Well, I never before knew anyone who went silent over some good feelings," Angie pointed out.

"They were good feelings, but there were bad ones mixed in," Peter corrected.

Angie was tracing designs on Peter's chest. He was stroking her arm.

"I've always been like that, Angie. It just happens suddenly, particularly on special occasions when I'm supposed to be extra happy. I can remember some of my birthdays . . ." Peter's voice trailed off.

"If birthdays are bad," Angie mused, "then what will Christmases be like with you? Do you go into your supersilent number?"

"Always. My folks used to get so upset. I seemed unappreciative, I guess."

Angie sighed at the prospect. "And all I wanted for Christmas was a man who'd talk."

"What a drag!" Peter replied, laughing. He blew a wisp of hair off Angie's forehead. "So tell me again about the job. Without all the extras this time."

"I'm laid off, as of today," Angie answered. "That's it. Mr. Ryan can't afford a countergirl. He'll handle the work himself."

"It was just a matter of time," Peter answered. "What do you want to do?"

"Look for another waitress job, I guess."

"How about trying something else? Want to be a salesclerk?"

"I'd like it in a pet shop."

"Let's have a look at the want ads." Peter got up and went to the living room.

"Want ads scare me," Angie confessed. "You read them. I'll get our dinner." She headed for the kitchen.

On the way to the couch, Peter detoured to Fog's box and picked up the kitten. Together, he and Fog thumbed and pawed their way through the Help Wanted columns.

"Gas station attendant?" Peter was reading out loud. "No, forget it. It's night shift only. Door-to-door salesperson? Forget that. Too uncertain. Janitorial helper?" Peter looked up from the paper. "No animal jobs, honey. Wait—'Marine World–Africa USA,' refreshment-stand helper."

"The only animals I'd see on that job would be impatient people with money in their hands. Besides, I'd use up all my earnings on transportation. I'll stick to coffee shops."

"You could phone around to the pet shops," Peter suggested.

"Let's not think about it now," Angie said. "Let's eat." She grinned as Peter sat down and spread Fog across his lap like a napkin.

With a twinkle in her eye, Angie struck a dramatic pose. "Like Scarlett O'Hara said in *Gone with the Wind,* 'I'll think about it tomorrow—at Tara. After all, tomorrow's another day.' "

"Hey, lady, I'm proud of you," Peter exclaimed. "You know *Gone with the Wind.* When did you read it?"

"Read it? Me? Come on! I saw the film. Four times."

Peter chuckled and looked down at Fog. "You heard the lady. She'll think about it tomorrow—at Tara."

Fog closed her eyes and went to sleep.

Angie was indeed thinking about the problem when she awoke the next morning. Catching the alarm before it went off, she lay in bed, weighing the job possibilities.

Peter stirred and opened his eyes. Seeing Angie's expression, he reached over to touch her.

"What are you looking so worried about?" he asked.

"My job, of course."

Peter yawned. "Come on, Angie. Losing that job isn't any big thing."

"Well, I think it's something. It's the only one I had."

Peter smiled at Angie's seriousness. He pulled her close.

"We'll survive, honey. We're living economically, you'll notice." He looked around at their few belongings. "Very economically! Someday we'll be fancier," he promised.

"There's no reason why I shouldn't help earn some

money, too," Angie told him. "You just watch me."

"Okay," Peter agreed, proud of his wife's spirit. "I'm president of your fan club." He gave Angie a friendly swat as he climbed out of bed. "Meanwhile, the gardens of our fair city are calling your husband."

"Where are you working now?"

"This week we're planting trees in the new Hubbard Avenue Park. Next week we'll plant the flower beds."

Angie put on her robe and went to start breakfast while Peter showered.

"I'm playing housewife today," she told Fog as she gave the kitten a morning hug. "I'll be around a bit until I find a new job."

Fog seemed satisfied with the arrangement.

Breakfast was quiet. Peter was wondering what kinds of trees he would be handling. Angie was trying to work out some sort of job-hunting strategy.

"You could drive me to work and have the car today," Peter suggested.

"Yeah, that would be good." Angie sounded casual. She didn't want to talk about her plans, because they were so confused. She didn't even want to think about her day. The uncertainty scared her.

Peter washed his dishes, then went to get ready to leave for work. Angie dressed quickly, her mind jumping from one possibility to the next.

When Peter seemed almost ready, Angie impulsively went to the closet and took out her quilted tote bag. Quickly she slipped Fog into the bag, putting a finger to her lips.

Fog melted down contentedly. When Angie reached into the bag and patted the furry head, a soft paw reached up to touch her wrist.

"We're going to take Peter to work," Angie whispered into the bag. She looked around to be sure Peter couldn't hear. "And then we're going to get me a job. Today . . . maybe . . . I wish."

Peter put on his jacket and picked up his keys.

"Ready?"

"Yes."

Angie went through the door sideways, keeping the arm with the tote bag out of Peter's sight. She glanced both ways down the walkway to make sure Mr. Rottweiler wasn't out mowing the lawn around the apartments. She clutched the handles of the bag nervously, glad when she finally reached the safety of the car.

To Angie's surprise, no sound and no movement came from the bag, even when she finally set it down on the car seat.

Peter glanced casually at the bag. "Your lunch?"

Angie choked on a laugh. "Good grief, I hope not!" She held the bag open for Peter to see.

"H'mm. Fog's legs for lunch, huh?" He chuckled to himself.

Angie gave Peter a poke. "I'm sure Fog thinks that's awful humor." She lifted the kitten out of the bag and set it on her lap.

Peter reached a hand over to scratch Fog's ear. At the same time, he also gave his wife's knee an affectionate pat.

"Your sins will be discovered, crazy lady. You know that, don't you? Are you going to drive around with a cat in your car and hope Mr. Rottweiler won't ever discover where the cat lives?"

"That's my plan," Angie replied calmly.

Smiling at Angie's seriousness, Peter shook his head. "Good luck with it."

As Angie and Peter pulled up in front of the maintenance yard, a dark-haired man in his mid-twenties was getting out of his parked van. He headed for the gate, then doubled back to pass near Peter's car.

"Hi there, Pete," he said, looking beyond Peter to size up Angie. "So that's your wife, huh? Wow!"

Angie exploded as the man moved on. "Who's that turkey? What's he mean, wow? I'm not a wow person. Nobody ever looks at me and thinks wow."

"Well, I think you're sort of wow," Peter said mildly, "so don't get so mad. That's Manny Schultz—and this is the first time I ever saw him show good taste in anything."

"Is he one of the city gardeners?"

"That's what he's paid to be. But from what I hear, the city doesn't see everything that Manny Schultz does while he's on the payroll."

"And you have to work with that guy?"

"I haven't yet, but my turn will come."

"Well, I hope today's not your unlucky day."

"So do I."

Peter leaned over to kiss Angie good-by. "Wow, Mrs. Ohlinger," he teased. "Wowee."

Angie gave her husband a playful shove. "Get out of here. Go plant a tree."

Peter got out of the car, and Angie slid over to the driver's seat.

"I'll pick you up at five o'clock," she called after him.

She waved and drove off, wondering about Manny Schultz. Was he like that with all the women?

Peter went into the office to check his duties for the day. Wonderful, he groaned inwardly as he looked at the work sheet. Guess who I get to plant trees with today.

32

Just then, Manny Schultz came over to the board to check his assignments.

"Well, old buddy," he said heartily, turning to Peter, "I see we'll be together today."

"Yeah," Peter replied flatly.

Manny had been with the city five years longer than Peter, so if they were assigned to a job together, Manny was in charge. He also had the advantage of feeling protected in his job, because his uncle was a city councilman.

Peter went out into the yard and waited for Manny to come around with the pickup truck.

"What's on our schedule?" Peter asked as he climbed into the truck. "Get our trees, first thing?"

"Number one, get a cup of coffee," was Manny's reply. "First things first."

Manny took a very long route to the park in order to stop at a coffee shop.

"Coming in?" he asked Peter.

"No, I'll just wait here."

Twenty-five minutes later, Manny emerged from the coffee shop and sauntered over to the truck. Peter looked at his watch, trying to hide his disgust.

"The nursery next, I guess," Manny announced without conviction.

On the way to the nursery, he stopped at the post office for stamps and at the market for cigarettes. Again Peter stared in disbelief at his watch.

At the nursery, the wholesaler loaded the pickup with the city's trees and shrubs and handed Manny the invoice for the order.

"Read me the list, will you?" Manny directed as he started the engine.

Peter read down the list. "Azaleas, rhododendrons, cedars (two kinds), redwoods, birches . . ."

"Stop there," Manny said. "How many birches? They would be nice."

"Fifteen," Peter told him. "What do you mean, 'They would be nice'?"

"I need to put something in the corner of my yard, and a couple of birches would be just right," Manny explained.

I don't believe this guy, Peter was thinking to himself. I just don't believe him. I've heard stories about him, and they're really true.

Manny stopped at his house and dropped off a pair of birch trees. Then, whistling, he drove to Hubbard Avenue Park.

"How do you handle it when the blueprints call for fifteen birches in the southwest corner and we plant thirteen?" Peter asked.

"You worry a lot, don't you?" Manny grumbled. "Who counts trees?"

Manny stopped the pickup at the southwest corner of the park. With the invoice in his hand, he hopped out and pointed to the place where the trees should be put. Peter unloaded the trees from the truck, while Manny made busywork for himself, checking each tree against the invoice.

"Good," Manny announced with a pleased smile. "All trees are accounted for." He marked the invoice "Order Complete." Then he sat down and lighted a cigarette.

He's got to be kidding, Peter thought. All trees are accounted for, but where can you find them if you should want to count?

After a twenty-minute cigarette break, Manny got

up and stretched. Then he started to measure off the locations of the trees.

"You bring them over," he told Peter, "while I mark where you should dig the holes."

Peter held out a shovel. "We have *two* shovels, Manny."

"Yeah, it's good to have a spare in case one breaks or gets misplaced," Manny replied breezily.

This guy has everything worked out, Peter marveled.

Manny's lunch break lasted an hour and a half. He left Peter at the park and went off in the truck, saying he was going to check something by phone with the maintenance yard.

At three o'clock, after a brief flurry of work on his part, Manny surveyed the finished area with satisfaction.

"Well, we did it!" he crooned. "We're quite a team. There's time to stop at home and watch a bit of the ball game on TV."

"We should call in and get another job to do," Peter pointed out. "We still have two hours."

"That would only rock the boat," Manny argued. "They're set up on one-day schedules. We just worked too fast today."

Unreal, Peter thought.

They loaded the tools into the truck, then Manny drove to his house.

"Now we can relax with a beer and the ball game," he sighed. "Come in and make yourself at home."

Peter knew he was in a bad spot. Everything up to this point had been misconduct on only Manny's part. Now Manny was asking Peter to break the rules with him.

No matter how Peter looked at it, the risks were high.

He was still a rookie in the department, and any mis-conduct on the job could get him fired. On the other hand, not joining Manny in his abuse of city time could turn Manny into an enemy. And Manny Schultz, with his political connections and his elastic conscience, would be a dangerous enemy. Either way, I'm in trouble, Peter concluded.

"Well," Manny demanded, "aren't you coming in?"

Manny was unlocking his front door. Peter was still sitting in the truck, stalling for time while he thought up an excuse.

"I feel uneasy about the way we left those trees," Peter told Manny. "The wind is coming up, and we didn't stake them."

"Like I said, you worry a lot," Manny replied.

"Why don't I go back and put the stakes in and tie the trees while you watch the game?" Peter suggested. "The stakes are already in the truck, anyhow."

"Come on!" Manny whined. "That's tomorrow's job. You want to give Frank crazy ideas about our work load?"

"This little bit won't impress anyone."

"Go ahead, if you want," Manny muttered. "Pick me up at four forty-five." He tossed the keys to Peter and went into his house.

Relieved, Peter drove back to the park, unloaded the stakes, and greeted his trees.

They're beautiful, Peter thought. What a spot this will be when it's finished! Lovingly, Peter drove a stake into the ground beside each tree, then talked to the tree as he tied it to the stake. When the job was finished, he sat on the ground and studied the layout of the park.

Without Manny in the picture, the scene looked very different to Peter. The disgust he felt for Manny and the frustration of being any part of Manny's operation began to fade as Peter sat alone, admiring the master landscaping plan. It's a little gem, he decided. Oh, how I'd love to design a park!

At four thirty, Peter left the park and headed for Manny's house. He honked and waited impatiently for Manny to appear.

True to form, Manny was in no hurry. After keeping Peter waiting for ten minutes, he strolled casually to the truck and motioned Peter to move over so he could drive.

When they were close to the maintenance yard, Peter spotted Angie and Fog sitting in the car near the gate. Manny honked and put his head out the window.

"Hey, hey, Mrs. Ohlinger," he shouted as he drove by.

Peter cringed, knowing what Angie was saying to herself.

When he opened the car door five minutes later, Peter was hit by a flood of Angie's comments about Manny Schultz. He climbed in and started the engine. Angie showed no signs of letting up.

"Hold it, honey. What are *you* sputtering about! I just spent eight hours working with that guy."

Peter looked to see if maybe that news would impress Angie. "No, on second thought, change that," he corrected. "I just spent eight hours working, while that guy put in about a two-hour workday."

Peter unloaded his pent-up feelings as he drove. "You wouldn't believe the stuff Manny Schultz pulls. He's unreal. Just listen to this . . ." Detail upon detail he told of Manny's ways of letting his partner do the work, of Manny's use of city time for personal activities, of Manny's method of acquiring city trees for his own garden. Manny—Manny—Manny, right up to their apartment building. Angie hadn't said a word since Peter had cut her off back at the maintenance yard.

When Peter stopped the car, Angie silently opened the door and got out, without even a glance at Peter. She stalked toward the apartment, never once looking back to see if Peter was even there.

Peter watched Angie in amazement. What's that all about? he wondered. What's with her?

FOUR

PETER, following behind Angie, caught up with her at the door to the apartment. As she fumbled in her purse for her key, he stepped forward and unlocked the door.

All the while, Angie kept her head turned away so as not to meet Peter's eyes.

Inside the apartment, Angie tossed her sweater on a chair and went right to Fog's box. She picked up the kitten and held it to her cheek, her back to Peter.

"What's wrong?" Peter asked.

Angie turned and walked away.

Peter washed up and then decided to try again. He found Angie sitting on the bed, stroking the sleeping kitten. A tear was rolling down each cheek.

"What is it, Angie? Tell me."

Angie got up and went into the kitchen. She put Fog back in her box and started fixing dinner. Peter would have loved to retreat into the five-thirty news, but he couldn't relax with things as they were.

Coming into the kitchen, he said, "Shall I fix the salad?"

Angie looked away.

"Okay, let's run through that one again. I will make a salad for our dinner."

Peter laid out the things from the refrigerator and went to work.

After a while, Angie set two plates of food on the table. Peter added two salads. The silent couple sat down to a silent dinner.

After a few bites, Peter said, "What was that you said once about my building walls of silence?"

Angie kept her eyes on her plate.

"Okay, what's wrong?" Peter said. His tone was firm.

"I didn't get thirteen jobs today, that's what's wrong!" Angie blurted out. Her voice trembled. "Thirteen jobs! Can you imagine it? Thirteen places advertised openings, and every single one was taken before I got there. It was a crummy day, Peter. I felt so awful. Then I waited for you at work, knowing that you would understand how I felt, even if no one else did. And what did you talk about all the way home? Manny Schultz. No 'How was your day, honey?' Just that Manny."

Angie finally looked straight at Peter. "Don't you care about my job? Don't I matter?"

"Don't you matter?" Peter tossed his fork onto his plate. "Don't I care? Angie, where do you get these crazy questions from?"

"Quit yelling at me."

"I'm not yelling at you. I'm yelling at those ridiculous ideas. What do you mean, don't you matter? I married you, didn't I?"

Angie rubbed her wedding band nervously. "It would be okay to tell me again," she said softly.

"I thought you knew it," Peter replied in a surprised tone.

"I kind of forget it when thirteen people turn me down in one day."

"Aw, Angie, they're only saying that the opening has been filled; they're not saying you're no good."

"Well, it seemed like I was no good after the first five. And by number thirteen, I really felt like some dumb little girl who didn't know anything."

"Not true! You don't even realize how nice you look and how well you handle things."

"Well, I didn't handle anything well today."

"That's because there was nothing to handle. A job opening that's been filled isn't much of a challenge."

"Yeah, that's true."

"Okay, now quit feeling like the puppy that was left outside in the cold, and tell me the places you went to."

Angie started counting them off on her fingers. "Three doughnut shops, four hamburger places, two delis, a gas station, a fabric shop, a health food store, and a restaurant. How's that for covering the field?"

"I'm impressed with you."

"Well, they weren't!"

"It's not you, honey; it's the economy. The jobs that used to go to young people are going to older people now. Women with kids are getting the jobs you were applying for."

"So what am I supposed to do? Get old? Have kids? Then apply again?"

Peter smiled at the mental picture. "Keep at it, I guess. Sooner or later, something will come your way."

Angie looked desolate. "I want a job, Peter."

"You'll get one."

By then, they both had finished dinner. Peter got up and took Angie's arm.

"Now, come with me, Mrs. Ohlinger. We're going to have a little talk."

He led her to the couch and pulled her down beside him.

"Although I don't see how you could wonder, I'm going to tell you again—I love you, Angie Ohlinger. I care about you. You matter to me more than anybody else in the world. And I married you because I want to spend my life with you."

Peter held Angie off at arm's length and looked her straight in the eye. "Are there any questions?"

Angie melted into his arms. "You couldn't possibly love me as much as I love you."

"Want to bet?"

"Peter, I'm sorry I acted like a baby about your not asking how my day was. Tell me about your day again. It may have been worse than mine, even."

"Well, the day itself wasn't that bad, really. But there's trouble wherever Manny Schultz is. He's got a lot of games going, and he expects the other guys to cover for him."

"I hate him," Angie said simply. "Next time I see him, I'll stick my tongue out at him!"

"That'll make a good person out of him," Peter said, laughing.

Then he looked at Angie with concern. "Seriously, though, be careful of him. Manny Schultz is bad news."

"I'm not scared of him."

"You'd better be," Peter warned. "Manny doesn't like what he calls straight arrows. And I can see what's coming. One of these days I'm going to be straight when he's crooked—and the mixture will explode."

"Come on," Angie said, snuggling up to Peter. "Let's go back to the part in the story where you were saying 'I love you, Angie.' "

"You like that story, huh?"

"Uh-huh."

"It's a bedtime story," Peter whispered with a wink. "So come with me, and we'll get on with the story."

Peter took Angie by the hand and led her to the bedroom.

Later that evening, when the kitchen was cleaned up, Angie and Peter sat down to relax in the living room. Peter reached for the daily newspaper. Angie reached for Fog.

"Now, let's look at these want ads in a new light," Peter said. He scanned the Help Wanted columns. "Hey, where did you find listings of the places you went today? They're not even in the paper."

"I drove around looking for Help Wanted signs in the windows," Angie replied.

Peter ran his finger down the column. "No, no, maybe, no, h'mm." His finger stopped at one listing. "That's the one to try, I'll bet." He tapped a spot in the want ads. "That's it. Why not go for the best? Forget the two-bit countergirls."

"What are you talking about?" Angie asked.

"Waitress, Camelot Inn."

"You're crazy. I'm not that good," Angie interrupted.

"Oh, but let me finish. 'Will train the right person,' it says."

"H'mm." Angie looked dreamy. "I've heard it's like a castle inside the Camelot, and the waitresses wear Old English costumes." She was lost in thought. "I couldn't possibly get that one. They'd want someone older than I am—maybe twenty-three or so."

"Go and put on your most grown-up outfit, and let's see how old you can look," Peter suggested.

Angie, thrilled that Peter was interested, dropped Fog onto his lap and hurried to the bedroom.

"Why don't you try that champagne-colored blouse my mother gave you for your birthday?" Peter called to her. "And your brown skirt. You have a nice jacket that goes with that skirt, haven't you?"

Angie appeared in a moment in nylons, heels, and the outfit Peter had suggested. Peter studied the effect.

"Nice," he murmured. "Very nice." Then he frowned. "But you look nineteen. A classy nineteen—but nineteen. I think it's the hair. Can you do anything else with your hair?"

Again Angie ducked into the bedroom. When she reappeared, she had her hair pulled back from her face, displaying the pearl earrings her parents had given her for her wedding.

Peter studied his wife. "As Manny Schultz would say, 'So that's your wife, huh? Wow!' "

Angie shook a fist at him.

"It's great," he said seriously. "Wear that."

Angie took off the outfit and hung it up carefully.

"I won't be able to sleep, I'm so nervous," she said.

Her day had been so tense, however, that she almost fell asleep half an hour later as they watched television on the couch.

Peter nudged his drowsy wife. "Do me a favor and go to bed, will you? I can't stay awake looking at you."

"Okay. You coming, too?" Angie asked, yawning as she shuffled toward the bedroom.

"Later. I want to watch the ten o'clock news first."

Angie flopped on the bed, barely managing to pull the covers over her before she was gone. The next thing she knew, the alarm was signaling six thirty.

For once, Angie was out of bed before the alarm ran down. She stopped the clanging and turned to look at her husband.

"Are you awake?"

"What for?" Peter cautiously opened one eye. "What makes you so bright-eyed at six thirty in the morning?"

"I'm going to get me a job today."

"Whoop-de-do! So you can bounce out of bed every morning at six thirty, huh?"

"Well, I guess I could work night shift. Get up after you leave; get home after you're in bed."

"And we could go for years without ever having to see each other."

"If I were married to Manny, I'd work it that way," Angie said.

"As a matter of fact, I think his wife does," Peter added. "And Manny has a rotating group of playmates who brighten his long and lonely evenings."

"He does?" Angie's eyes widened. "Where does Manny find women who can stand him?"

Peter shrugged and headed for the shower. Angie dressed quickly and went to start breakfast.

"I'll ride with you to work," she called, "and then take the car. Okay?"

Peter came into the kitchen, buttoning his shirt. "Sure," he replied with a twinkle in his eye. "That way you can smile at Manny as he arrives for work."

Angie stuck out her tongue at Peter, and then shoved a plate of eggs and toast into his hands.

When it was time to leave, Angie put Fog into the tote bag. "It's all right," she assured Peter. "I'll be coming back to the apartment. I want to phone for an appointment for an interview."

Peter smiled at his wife, and pulled the apartment door closed. He stood for a moment, studying his potted bamboo.

Angie, looking down the walkway, noticed the landlord pruning the shrubs by the next building. She nudged Peter.

"There's Mr. Rottweiler," she whispered. "Should I go back inside?"

"No, just keep calm," Peter advised her. "Look innocent as you walk by him."

Angie held the tote bag closer to her as they approached the landlord.

Mr. Rottweiler straightened up to greet them. His manners were polite and formal—old European. "Lovely morning," he said, smiling.

"Beautiful," Peter agreed. "Those shrubs are looking fine."

"Thank you, Peter." Then, turning to Angie, he asked, "And how are you this morning?" He nodded at her tote bag. "Going shopping, I see."

Angie gulped. "After I drop Peter off at work," she replied weakly.

Fog, inside the bag, changed positions. The bag moved slightly. Quickly, Angie transferred it to her other arm.

"Well, have a good day," Peter told the landlord. He took Angie's trembling arm to steady it. When he did so, Fog meowed. Peter coughed to cover the sound. As they hurried down the walk, Angie whispered, "Do you think we're in trouble?"

"I don't think so," Peter replied. "But that was too close for comfort."

"I was scared to death," Angie confessed. "What if he had caught us?"

She was still trembling when they reached the car. She rode silently all the way to the maintenance yard, her thoughts gradually turning from Fog to jobs. I sure hope I can get an appointment for today, she kept thinking. I sure hope.

When Peter stopped the car at the maintenance yard entrance, Angie finally spoke. "I'm so nervous I won't last till tomorrow."

Peter patted her knee. "Well, good luck," he said, "in case you do survive."

He leaned over to kiss Angie. A knock on the car window startled them both.

"Hey, hey, hey, Mrs. Ohlinger!" Manny crooned. He wagged a finger at Fog. "What's new, pussycat?"

"Drop dead, creep!" Angie muttered under her breath.

Peter, amused, shook a warning finger at Angie. "Remember, you're supposed to be twenty-three today. Twenty-three-year-old waitresses at the Camelot Inn do not tell people to drop dead."

"What do they say—Will you kindly expire?" Angie grinned as Peter walked away from her.

She hurried home to the phone, only to find she couldn't get a call in before nine o'clock. When she did get an answer, she was told to come for an interview anytime between ten and twelve.

"I'll beat them all," Angie promised Fog. "I'll make the first impression."

She dashed for the shower, dressed quickly, and then spent a long time on her hair and face. Just enough makeup to look mature, ladylike, Old English? Angie didn't really know what impression she was trying to give. She just wanted the job.

With a final glance in the mirror, she turned to Fog. "Here goes. Would you hire me?"

Fog's chin rested on her paws. Her tail flicked in response. Angie tossed the cat a wave and closed the apartment door.

The high heels made a difference as Angie moved toward the car. She found herself walking in a new way. More elegantly, she told herself.

When she arrived at the Camelot Inn, Angie tried to get out of the car gracefully. Someone might be watching, she thought. Look twenty-three, she reminded herself. Act twenty-three.

Angie threaded her way through the corridors of the Camelot Inn to the room in the back where interviews were being held. Pausing at the door, she straightened her skirt, took a deep breath, and stepped in.

A secretary handed her an application form and told her she would be twelfth in the interviews.

As Angie waited to be called, she studied the other applicants. I'm certainly the youngest, she thought. Peeking at the applications near her, Angie noticed things like fifteen and twenty years of experience.

Some of the women are nice-looking, she decided, and some look like tough old pros. But next to all of them, I look like a kid. A nice kid, maybe, but a kid.

When Angie's turn came, she stood up carefully in her high heels, walked into the interviewing room— gracefully, she hoped—and sat down without crossing her knees. She had read somewhere that you look better in an interview with your ankles crossed, tucked back a little under the chair.

"Hello, Angie," the interviewer began. He was scanning her application. "I'm Luigi Gaviota. I supervise the

48

dining room staff. You can call me Luigi."

Angie burst out laughing. "I come to Camelot's Old English dining room, and find it's run by a Luigi. What happened to the Archibalds and the Chaunceys?" Then she clapped her hand to her mouth, horrified at her lack of dignity.

"Archibald and Chauncey lost out to Luigi because this Italian knows how to keep his help happy." Luigi winked at Angie.

"Now, Angie, tell me about your experience in fancy dining rooms."

"I've only worked in a café," Angie replied, worrying that her confession might end the interview. "But the ad said you'd train the right person."

"So what makes you the right person to train, Angie?"

"Oh, I'll do anything you want done."

Luigi smiled broadly at Angie.

"I'm a hard worker. And I learn fast."

"Our waitresses work in costume, you know," Luigi continued. "How do you feel about that?"

"It sounds beautiful," Angie bubbled. "I'd like that."

"We start our trainees on breakfast and lunch only," Luigi explained.

"That would be ideal. Then I wouldn't have to be at work when my husband's at home."

"Does your husband approve of your applying for this job, Angie?"

"Yes, he says anything I'm happy with is okay with him."

"While you're training, you may have to stay sometimes beyond the set hours. Can you handle that?"

"Just give me a chance to show you what I can do, and I'll work out everything," Angie promised.

"Well, Angie . . ." Luigi put a hand on her knee. "I have to finish a lot more interviews. We'll contact you by phone when the decision has been made." Luigi patted Angie's knee, running his hand up her leg just a little. "Thank you for coming in, dear."

"Thank you." Angie gave Luigi what she hoped was an Old English smile as she left.

What was that hand-on-the-knee bit? Angie wondered as she wound her way back out of the castle. What kind of interviewers do fancy restaurants have?

I hope Luigi's just a nice fatherly Italian, she thought. He said he keeps his help happy.

Angie went straight home from the interview. She knew it could be a week before she heard anything, but she wanted to be sure she didn't miss the call, anyhow.

Her heels clicked along the walkway as she hurried from the car to the apartment. Mr. Rottweiler, standing high on a ladder, cleaning out rain gutters, smiled down at her.

"Good afternoon, Angie," he called.

"Hello, Mr. Rottweiler," she called back with a wave.

I really should wave with both hands, Angie thought to herself. Just to show him. See, Mr. Landlord, I'm clean. Go on and search me with your X-ray eyes. I'm innocent. For once, she added with a chuckle.

Inside the apartment, Angie gathered up Fog and settled herself on the bed by the phone. She dozed off, dreaming of herself in an Old English costume. When she opened her eyes and looked at the clock, she jumped up in horror.

"Oh no," she groaned, "Peter's been waiting thirty minutes for me to pick him up."

Angie dashed to the car and rushed to the maintenance yard.

Peter was tired and hungry, and he had had a bad day with Manny.

"How come you're so late?" he muttered as he climbed into the car.

"I was hoping to get a phone call from the Camelot Inn," Angie replied, knowing it was a flimsy excuse. "Sorry you had to wait."

Peter didn't pursue the subject. He seemed absorbed in his own thoughts.

"I didn't hear from them yet." Angie looked at Peter for some response. "But I think the interview went pretty well."

Peter wasn't listening. Angie knew she was talking to herself.

"I found out that the waitresses actually do wear Old English costumes." Angie's voice became higher and louder as she tried to get Peter's attention. "And the trainees work only at breakfast and lunch—no dinners. It sounds perfect."

"That's good," Peter said absently.

"What did I just say?" Angie asked.

"Something is perfect."

Angie gave up on the conversation. The rest of the trip home was silent.

She had been home all afternoon, but hadn't even started dinner. She had been dreaming by the telephone. This didn't go over very well with Peter, whose day had used up all his patience.

"That's a great-looking dinner you fixed," he commented sarcastically.

Angie couldn't think of any safe answer to that one.

The two of them tripped over each other in the small kitchen, trying to throw together a quick meal. Then just as they finally sat down to eat, the phone rang.

Angie didn't react immediately. Then it dawned on her. She jumped up and grabbed the phone.

"Yes . . . Yes . . . Oh, hi, Luigi . . . You did? . . . You do? . . . Great . . . When? . . . Sure . . . Uh-huh, I liked you, too, Luigi. Thanks a lot . . . Okay, see you tomorrow."

"Yippee!" Angie flopped down on the chair at the table, her arms flying into the air.

"Who's this Luigi?" Peter asked grumpily. "What's this 'I liked you, too' business?"

"Luigi is my new boss."

"Luigi? A Luigi runs an Old English dining room? What happened to the Englishmen?"

"They got fired and Luigi got hired because he keeps his help happy, he says."

"That I gotta see."

"Don't be such a grouch. Luigi is a nice, kind, fatherly sort."

"Yeah, I've seen that type in operation."

Angie threw up her hands in exasperation. "Can't you be a little thrilled? I just got me a really good job, and you don't care at all."

"I care," Peter protested feebly.

"No one would ever know it. What's wrong with you tonight?"

"I've really had it today. I've had it up to here with Manny. I can't react to one more thing." Peter pushed his chair back from the table. "I'm going to lie down."

Peter headed for the bedroom. At the doorway, he turned to look at Angie.

"No, I'm not shutting you out. Yes, I do care about your job. I'm just exhausted."

Angie, suddenly realizing how little she had sensed of her husband's mood, felt terrible.

"I'm sorry I was babbling on," she apologized. "I'll tell you about the job tomorrow."

She quickly cleared the table and tidied up the kitchen. Then she stood in the bedroom doorway, wondering if Peter was asleep.

"Want me to rub your back?" she whispered.

"Love it," Peter mumbled, his face buried in the pillow.

Angie got some lotion and smoothed it over Peter's shoulders and back. "Do you want to tell me about your day?" she asked softly as she massaged the tense muscles.

"Some other time."

Angie worked quietly until she thought Peter was asleep. She closed the lotion bottle and started to tiptoe away.

Peter's arm reached out for her. "Aren't you going to lie down with me?"

Angie melted onto the bed.

"So you're a little Old English waitress now," Peter mumbled. "Congratulations."

Angie lifted her head to answer. Peter was sound asleep.

Although Peter slept soundly all night, Angie was too excited to relax. Finally, she gave up trying and went into the bathroom to experiment with ways to wear her hair. I'll bet the costumes have those little lacy caps, she thought. I might even have my hair trimmed a bit on the sides in front.

She turned slowly, studying her figure in the mirror. Hardly a knockout, she decided, but pretty good. The Old English style is tight-fitting down to the waist, I think, and I'm okay down to that point.

After a while, Angie went back to bed, sleeping restlessly till morning.

"Feeling better this morning?" she asked Peter when he finally stirred.

"I guess so. I really couldn't feel much worse than I did last night." Peter lifted his head to test the day. "Honey, did you tell me last night that you got the job at Camelot Inn?"

"That's right. Starting today," Angie replied with a smug little smile.

"You'll be great. I can see why they would grab you fast."

Angie cringed. "Don't say that. I'd like to be hired, not grabbed."

She was remembering, with just a little anxiety, Luigi's winks and his hand on her knee.

As they went about their morning tasks, both Angie and Peter were busy with their own thoughts. Breakfast passed without any conversation.

Finally Peter spoke as he picked up his dishes to take them to the sink. "Are you going to need the car to get there?"

"That's another good thing," Angie replied happily. "I found that the Camelot Inn is on a direct bus line from here—every twenty minutes."

"It sounds too good to be true."

"Doesn't it?"

Secretly, Angie had a good feeling about the way she seemed to have impressed Luigi. She knew he had picked her because he thought she was young and bouncy.

"Well, you have a happy day, honey." Peter kissed Angie good-by. "Unfortunately, I'll be having another awful one with Manny."

"I thought you only had to work with him now and then."

"Since we started planting the Hubbard Avenue Park together, and since the work has been going so well with us as a team—according to the foreman—we are scheduled to complete the park together. Isn't that wonderful?"

"If you have a happy foreman, and if the park is looking good, what's so terrible?" Angie asked.

"Manny Schultz is stealing the city blind. He's short-changing them on working time by two to three hours a day. And I'm doing all that work that looks so good. That's all that's wrong."

Angie thought steam might begin to pour from her husband's ears. She rubbed his shoulders comfortingly.

"Well, I'll massage your back when the day is over. That's about all I can think of to help." Angie sighed. "Isn't there someway to get that guy?"

"My big worry right now is keeping that guy from getting me!" Peter said. "Every day I'm witness to more and more of his activities. And every day he gets more and more worried that I won't continue to cover for him indefinitely. I could blow the whistle on him so easily . . . except"—Peter turned very serious—"except that Manny Schultz will try to get me before I get him. I know how he figures."

Angie shivered, as if a storm cloud had just threatened her bright sunny day. She tried to recapture her joyous, excited mood, but the black cloud kept hanging over her.

FIVE

ANGIE and Peter were poor company for each other when they got together that evening at dinnertime.

Angie was bubbling with enthusiasm, eager to share all the little details of her new job. Peter was tight-jawed, tense, and furious.

"Our costumes are made of adorable little-print cotton, and have long full skirts," Angie crooned. "And the tops—they're cut low at the neckline. I mean they're *low*, Peter. I was so embarrassed when I first put the dress on. But Luigi said it looked great."

"What's Luigi doing? Sitting there watching you try on your costume?" Peter asked sourly.

"No, silly. But he's in charge of the whole effect we make in the dining room. So he's got to know how our costumes fit."

Peter didn't really care about the explanation. He just needed to squelch the enthusiasm. Someone who had had a happy day was really hard for him to deal with at that moment.

"And it's dark in the dining room." Angie raced on. "We have little candles on every table. And you should see the beautiful food we serve. Oh, it's so elegant."

56

"And I suppose you had that elegant food for your lunch?" Peter was ready to resent anything that had been pleasant.

"Oh no, trainees would have to pay for that food. I just had a cheese sandwich and a carton of milk from the machine in the employees' lounge."

Angie glanced at Peter and noticed for the first time his dark and angry expression.

"You had a rotten day, huh?"

"That's a polite way of putting it."

"Manny again?"

"Naturally."

Peter was silent for a while. Then he spoke, as if he were reciting it all to himself.

"That guy took a four-hour lunch break today. 'I have to tend to some business,' he says, and he drives off in the city truck. From eleven to three he's gone. And I'm planting the park alone. No explanation. No apology. As if it's perfectly normal behavior on the job."

"For him, I guess it is," Angie remarked. Then she hoped her comment didn't sound frivolous when Peter was so angry.

"I just wish I knew what that guy does when he takes those long lunch hours . . ." Peter's voice trailed off.

Angie cleared the table and did the dishes. All the while, Peter sat at the table brooding.

Finally, Angie decided to take a hand.

"That guy's poison," she pointed out. "You know that, don't you?" She paused to see if Peter would acknowledge that fact. "You need to get him out of your system." She was still waiting for some reaction. "Come on, why don't we go for a walk along the Ridge Trail?"

"I don't think I want to move," Peter replied with a sigh. "I've been moving all day."

"I know. Doing the work of two people."

"Right."

"So trust me," Angie urged. "The wind off the ocean and the long views out to sea are good medicine."

Angie tugged on Peter's arm until he finally began to move. She got his windbreaker and held it up while he slipped into it. Then she put on her own jacket as Peter picked up his keys and headed for the door.

"Wait a minute," Angie said. "Hold everything."

She took her tote bag from the closet and put Fog into it. "Okay, we're ready."

Peter shook his head and smiled faintly at his wife and her furry friend. They walked toward the car, acting as casual as if the bag contained a package of cheese and two apples.

Then just as Angie began to breathe freely, an apartment door opened, and the landlord stepped out, carrying some paint cans.

"Oh, good evening, Peter and Angie."

"Good evening, Mr. Rottweiler." Peter nudged Angie to respond, too. She couldn't find her voice, but she managed a little wave.

"Going out for a pleasant evening?"

"A walk on the Ridge Trail," Peter told him.

The landlord turned to Angie. "I hope you have an extra wrap in your bag. It's going to be quite chilly tonight."

Angie clutched the tote bag tighter. "Oh yes," she managed to reply.

"Well, good night." Mr. Rottweiler walked off with his paint cans.

Angie stood there, watching the landlord turn a corner. "Peter," she said, trembling, "did you see how he stared at my bag?"

"You're just paranoid, Angie."

"He did stare at it, Peter. I swear. Those X-ray eyes went right through the bag and saw Fog."

Peter gave Angie a little hug and led her to the car. "Forget about it, honey. Mr. Rottweiler was very polite. That's just his way. I like him."

"Well, he makes me nervous."

"I know," Peter said, laughing. He opened the car door and let Angie in.

As they drove off, Angie took Fog from the bag and let the kitten lie on her lap. Fog had been riding in cars ever since Angie had brought her home, and she was perfectly at ease with moving wheels.

Peter reached over and rubbed Fog's chin. Then he glanced at Angie.

"Hey, you worked all day, too," he said. "How come you aren't exhausted?"

"Mine was a good day, so it didn't do me in like yours," Angie replied. "Remember, you were never very tired when you didn't have to work with Manny. It's the people who are tough to handle, not the plants."

"It's not even people," Peter pointed out. "It's person. One. Only one. The rest of the gardeners are okay."

"Hold it!" Angie warned. "We're going out to get away from Manny."

"I keep forgetting. All right, let's put Manny in cold storage for now."

"Good. And let's lock the freezer door."

"And turn down the temperature. Way, way down."

"Bye, Manny." Angie waved a solemn farewell.

Together, they chuckled at the mental image of

Manny disappearing into the deepfreeze.

The route to the Ridge Trail went past the entrance to the Crestline Community College campus. Peter, lost in thought, reacted after he had passed the gate. He braked suddenly and backed up.

"What are you doing?" Angie wanted to know.

"Let's drive through the campus and see what the Landscape Design department is up to at this season."

"Okay," Angie reluctantly agreed, "but let's not get sidetracked and miss our walk."

Peter followed the loop road around the campus, finally stopping by a fenced enclosure. A sign on the gate said, "The Corner Park—Endowed by the A. G. Putnam Foundation, and Maintained by the Landscape Design Students of Crestline College."

Peter got out to see if the gate was unlocked, and then returned to Angie.

"Honey, this place is so nice, it's worth seeing." There was an excitement in Peter that Angie hadn't seen for a while. "Students try out their best designs here; and there are some beauties."

"All right, go ahead and take a look if you want to," Angie said without much enthusiasm. She studied her watch, figuring the amount of daylight left. Her plan for a romantic walk in the sunset was rapidly getting away from her.

"I meant, let's look at it together." Peter held out a hand for her. "We have it all to ourselves tonight."

"I wanted to walk the Ridge Trail," Angie protested. "And see the sunset."

"We'll get to that. This'll only take a minute." Peter's eyes were pleading with Angie. "Come on, honey. I walk around in a park alone all day. Tonight I want to share a park with my wife."

I knew I'd lose, Angie said to herself, half sorry and half pleased. Peter, with his outstretched hand, was so appealing that Angie couldn't resist him.

She got out of the car with Fog in her arms.

"Here, I'll take her," Peter said.

He took the kitten and lifted her up to his shoulder, then draped her around his neck like a fur collar. Fog tensed for a moment, then relaxed comfortably. Peter kept both his hands on the kitten until he was sure she felt secure. Then he reached for Angie's hand.

As they moved from one student's garden to another, Peter pretended to be taking snapshots.

"And this is a picture of the Peter Ohlinger family strolling in the Corner Park," he chanted.

"And this is a picture of the Peter Ohlinger family admiring a *Metasequoia glyptostroboides.*

"And this is a picture of the Ohlinger cat—no, forget that one." Peter quickly put his hand in front of Fog's eyes.

Angie looked at Peter quizzically.

"Why did we forget that one?"

"I didn't want Fog to look at the Japanese carp pond. She's too young to be thinking about fishing."

By then, Angie was completely charmed. She giggled at the idea of the big man guarding the tiny kitten's innocence.

They paused in an area fragrant with roses.

"And this is a picture of Peter Ohlinger kissing his wife in the rose garden."

Peter pulled Angie close and gave her a long, lingering kiss. Then he straightened his living fur collar.

Dusk was gradually shifting to darkness. The colors became softer, the breezes gentler, the fragrance of the flowers more intense. Angie's and Peter's voices became whispers.

The path led from one area to the next, each a miniature park with a distinct style of its own.

Looking like honeymooners, Angie and Peter strolled along, their arms around each other's waists. Angie thought fleetingly of her original plan and chuckled. I wanted to walk the Ridge Trail because it would be romantic? Crazy me. I had no idea what Peter was like in the Corner Park.

Peter, his eyes sparkling, quietly pointed out features of each garden, explaining how he would have done things.

In the farthest corner, the path led to a secluded area, separated from the rest of the garden by a wall of bamboo. Polished stones, mosses, and dwarf pines surrounded a small grassy mound.

"Now, this one is just to my taste." Peter was entranced. "They knew I was coming!"

He dropped onto the grassy mound and pulled Angie down beside him. Setting Fog on the lawn beneath the young cherry tree, he said, "You practice your tree-climbing while your mother and I discuss some matters of importance."

Then Peter took Angie in his arms.

"And this picture . . . ," he murmured after the first few kisses, "this picture is censored."

The tiny park became their own. For a while, every sound belonged only to Angie and Peter. A rustling leaf, an insect's hum, a bird's chirp.

Gradually they drifted into private worlds, neither intruding on the other's thoughts. They remained that way for a long time—close in body, miles apart in thought.

All the while, the sky was darkening. The pattern of the leaves became a blur. The ground grew cold.

At that point, Peter pulled himself back to some kind of reality. He stood up reluctantly, plucked Fog from the tree, and offered Angie a hand.

Reentry into the real world was slow. Angie and Peter walked in silence back to the car. As he started the engine and turned on the headlights, Peter spoke.

"We didn't make it to the Ridge Trail, did we?"

"I think we got sidetracked." Angie snuggled close to her husband, resting her arm on his leg and patting his knee with her hand. She could sense how much at peace with himself Peter had been in that park setting. At peace with her, too.

Angie noticed Peter glancing at her. "So you like being in a park with your wife, do you?" she asked teasingly. "Better than being in a park with Manny?"

Peter kept his eyes on the road, but Angie could see traces of a smile as he answered.

"Well, there are lots of things Manny can do that you can't."

"Like what?" Angie demanded. "I could drive a truck, plant flowers, prune trees, drive a power mower . . ."

"Yeah, but can you lie and steal?"

"Okay," Angie conceded. "Manny can do more than I can."

"H'mm, not necessarily *more.*" Peter's tone softened. "But definitely different. I guess I'd choose you over Manny. Yeah . . . I think I would."

They rode home in comfortable silence.

While she was waiting to fall asleep that night, Angie ran through the scene in the Corner Park one more time, savoring each detail. Somehow it had been different from any of the other sentimental moments she and Peter had shared. Part of the time he wasn't even thinking about me, Angie recalled. And yet, I've never felt more loved.

What do you know, she thought with surprise. The honeymoon must be over. We're into marriage.

"Hey, Peter! Guess what?"

Peter had fallen asleep. Angie couldn't share her discovery.

What do you suppose he was thinking about? Angie wondered. He was different in that setting. Really different.

Then Angie began to realize something she had only casually acknowledged before. Peter has another love besides me. Landscaping does something for him that I can't do. I'm always going to have to share my man with a tree, a flower, a lawn.

She reached one foot over to feel Peter's warmth. She put her hand under his. And then she fell asleep.

For Angie, the night was filled with restless dreams. Manny was there, making trouble on the job. She was there, trying not to lean too far over in her low-cut waitress costume. And Peter was there, saying, "Meet me in the park, Angie."

Angie awakened at two thirty. There was something she had to think through. What really happened in the Corner Park last night? she kept wondering. It was as if we had put the last piece into a jigsaw puzzle and suddenly the picture was complete. Landscape design must be the name of that missing piece in Peter. With it, he's complete and content.

Angie was impressed with her new insight. I wonder if Peter knows what I know. I'll bet he doesn't. He thinks he can't afford to go to college, now that he's married. Well, I'm going to show him what married people can do, Angie promised herself in the darkness. I'm going to earn the money to keep us going while he goes to school. I've even got the job to do it. I'll become a superduper Old English waitress and make fabulous tips.

At peace with her decision, Angie dropped off into restful sleep.

SIX

ANGIE woke the next morning, hugging her plans. I'm not going to talk about college yet, she decided. I'll just go ahead and get good at my job, and as soon as I'm earning steady money, I'll suggest that Peter start the Landscape Design program at Crestline.

Angie hummed softly as she moved through the breakfast routine. Peter was quiet. Angie couldn't tell what he was thinking.

When she passed him while he was sitting at the breakfast table, Peter reached out an arm and pulled her onto his lap. For a moment he buried his face in her hair, and then let her go with a friendly swat on the seat.

Peter wasn't talking, but this time it didn't worry Angie. She knew exactly what she was going to do. Her new job was the key to everything.

She would succeed beyond Luigi's highest expectations. Soon all the regular customers would ask to sit at one of Angie's tables. They would tip handsomely. And she would bring the money home and say, "See, Peter, you can go to school now, and I'll keep the money coming in."

Peter, unaware of Angie's new goal, viewed her work casually. He figured the job wasn't so good as Angie believed it was. But if she was happy, fine.

"Have a good day at work," he said as she put on her jacket and got ready to leave. He wished he could face his own day with the same enthusiasm.

While Peter drove to work, he tried to prepare himself for another day with Manny. As he pulled up at the maintenance yard, Manny was locking his car.

"Hi there, Pete," he called. "Where's the little woman today?"

"Working." The conversation died there.

Manny was not in a good mood. Peter could see that right away as they drove to the Hubbard Avenue Park.

The morning was filled with Manny's obscenities. Obscenities for the truck, which stalled because he drove it so badly. Obscenities about the wholesaler, who didn't have the order quite ready for pickup. Obscenities for the flowers because there were so many of them to be planted.

The day's planting was to be done along a one-way road that wound through the park. In order to have the supplies near the site, it was necessary to block the road to traffic. Manny didn't think about that problem until they were already started on the job.

Manny let out another barrage of obscenities as he realized he had messed up again. Grudgingly, he lifted a barricade from the truck and started to walk back down the road with it.

"You keep unloading plants," Manny called to Peter over his shoulder. "I'll take this thing back to the intersection."

"And why not?" Peter mumbled. "Old Pete can keep on lifting dirt, while Manny takes an hour to carry his little barricade a quarter of a mile."

Manny sloppily plunked the barricade down at the intersection, without ever considering how a driver would interpret it. There was no ROAD CLOSED sign, no warning, nothing but a small barricade sitting off-center in the road, with room for a car to pass right by.

It was like a spider in its web awaiting a victim—only a matter of time before an unsuspecting driver would fall into the trap.

Within a half hour it was all happening. A nice-looking woman in a stylish little car wound her way along the one-way road, looking for a good spot to run her dog. Rounding a bend, she found herself face-to-face with the city truck and a road full of plants.

Before she could even size up the situation and put her car in reverse, she was assaulted by a barrage of Manny's obscenities, ending with the question, "Don't you even know what a road barricade means? Why don't you learn to drive, you dumb broad!"

Peter, horrified, turned his back and began to dig furiously, as if he wanted to make a hole and crawl into it.

The woman slammed her car in reverse and it careened back down the road. Manny, now sullen and silent, turned to the plants. He climbed onto the truck bed and began wildly tossing everything off the truck onto the road. Plants went flying. Tools clattered to the pavement. A bag of manure split open.

"Manny," Peter shouted, "what the devil are you doing? Are you crazy?"

He raced over to rescue some plants.

By then, the truck was empty. Manny climbed into the cab, tossed Peter's lunch out, and ground away at the starter. When it caught, he gunned the engine and shot off. Peter, knocked off-balance by the lurching truck, flattened several flats of flowers as he landed. He eased himself off the plants onto the road, trying to straighten up a few bent stems as he collected his thoughts.

"That guy's crazy," Peter said to the flowers.

Many of the plants were too damaged to use, but Peter went to work getting the good ones into the ground. Finally, there was nothing left on the road except a litter of mangled plants, broken pots, and spilled manure.

When Peter looked up from his planting, he saw a city car coming down the road. It stopped near the litter, and the supervisor of parks got out.

"Hello, Mr. Rivlin," Peter said, wiping his dirty hands on his pants.

"What happened out here this morning?" Mr. Rivlin asked.

"Well, what have you heard so far?" Peter asked.

"That some gardener working in Hubbard Avenue Park verbally assaulted the wife of a city councilman this morning."

"Oh no!" Peter groaned. "She was a councilman's wife?"

"Yes, and she's furious. And the councilman is furious. And together, they plan to give us a lot of trouble."

"Whew! Manny's the nephew of another councilman, too, isn't he?" Peter added.

"Just to make things even stickier." Mr. Rivlin sighed. "Why don't you tell me exactly what happened?"

Peter gave the supervisor a full account of his morning.

Then Mr. Rivlin looked directly at Peter and said, "I

know being an informer is a bad role to have to play, but the department must protect itself. Are you aware of any other misconduct on the part of Manny Schultz?"

"H'mm," Peter mused. "Where do I begin? What do you already know? Have you tallied the tool check-out and check-ins? You'll find a lot missing. Have you made a count of trees planted compared with the invoices from the wholesalers? You'll find you're short trees. Have you checked lunch-hour activities? Manny's time schedule has been very leisurely. Have you looked for Manny on the job when a ball game's on TV? He's easy to find—in his living room."

Mr. Rivlin shook his head. "Manny sounds like a real winner."

"Working with him is an experience," Peter agreed. "One I could do without."

"As of right now, you'll be without him," the supervisor said, getting into his car. "Manny Schultz will be suspended pending investigation. I'll send someone else out with a truck to pick you up."

"Thanks. That'll be refreshing."

"It sounds as if you've had more than your share of Manny."

"It's been plenty," Peter agreed with a grin.

Mr. Rivlin backed his car away from the litter and disappeared around the bend. Peter returned to his job of salvaging plants.

By midafternoon the planting was finished and the roadway cleared. The trash was in a pile, the tools lined up beside the road. Peter sat down to admire his first-aid job on the injured flowers. In spite of Manny's touch, the park was beginning to look great.

A maintenance truck rattled to a stop and a young

woman in work clothes climbed out.

"Hi, Carrie," Peter said, getting up from the ground. "What brings you here?"

"I just got reassigned. I'm supposed to help you finish the park planting." She glanced at Peter hesitantly. "I hope you don't mind working with the only woman gardener in the department."

"You're a welcome relief, Carrie. I've heard from the other guys that you're a good gardener and you carry your work load."

"Well, Manny Schultz didn't think so. I worked with him for one day, and he complained to the foreman about me."

"Take it as a compliment, Carrie. To be disliked by Manny is something of an honor."

Carrie grinned. "I hear you're number one on his hit list now, Peter. He was furious that you didn't cover for him today."

"Yeah, probably."

Peter tried to sound casual, but deep down he knew there was nothing casual about Manny's fury.

"Why don't you show me what's been done, and what we still have ahead of us," Carrie suggested.

So Peter gave Carrie a tour of the park, pointing with pride to the areas that he had planted. Other crews would be coming in for nonplanting jobs, but Peter felt he had given the park its soul.

Carrie was enthusiastic. She liked the planting that had been done so far. She thought the rest of the plans sounded wonderful. She looked forward to starting on the park the next morning.

How did I get so lucky? Peter thought as they headed back to the maintenance yard. Talk about extremes— I think I've gone from the nastiest to the pleasantest member of the maintenance crew in one day.

When they pulled into the yard, Carrie left Peter with a smile and a wave. A group of men gathered around Peter to get the firsthand account of Manny's mistake.

"He was smoldering like a volcano all morning," Peter told them. "And then, just like that, he went up in smoke over a silly little incident—a woman didn't see his barricade and drove down the blocked road."

"He picked the wrong woman to yell at," one of the men remarked.

"I hear that lady is out to get his hide," another added.

"Yeah, I hear she wants it made into a rug for their den."

"So she can walk on it for the next twenty years."

"Whew! So long, Manny."

"It couldn't have happened to a nicer guy."

Everyone laughed.

Peter kept wondering where Manny was. His name was on everyone's lips, but Manny was nowhere to be seen.

"He's sure got you on his hate list," one of the men told Peter.

"Well, how did he think I could cover for him when he stood there shouting obscenities at a lady in a car?"

"Manny doesn't think, Peter. That's the answer."

"By the way, I hear you'll be working with Carrie instead" one of the men commented to Peter as they walked toward the office. "Lucky you. But we can't resent that. You've kept Manny off the rest of our backs all this time."

"Yeah, I deserve a break," Peter admitted.

As he drove home, Peter kept wondering what

Manny would do to get back at him. Put a bomb in his car? No, too dramatic and obvious. Engineer an accident? No, too risky. Basically, Manny's a chicken.

Peter chuckled as his mind wandered. You know who'll miss him most? Angie. When there's no more "Hey, hey, Mrs. Ohlinger" and "What's new, pussycat?" who will there be for her to hate so fervently?

In a way, Peter felt freed. No more Manny. He chose not to think about what further dealings he might have with the man. For the moment, at least, he felt a great sense of relief.

Angie was cooking dinner when Peter unlocked the apartment door. She took a quick look over her shoulder and offered a casual "Hi."

"Ta da. Attention! Attention! Red-hot press release!"

Angie, not sure what was going on, turned to face Peter.

"News item: Fans of Manny Schultz will mourn the cancellation of the popular daytime show, *Manny Schultz, Wonder Gardener.*" Peter changed his tone to sound like a funeral director. "You, Mrs. Ohlinger, his special admirer, surely will miss him most of all. My condolences, madam."

Angie stood there, holding a knife and a dripping carrot.

"You want to say that again? In plain English?"

"He blew it. He got canned."

"You're kidding."

"Nope. No kidding. Well, actually, he's not fired until after the investigation. But he's on suspension as of noon today. And the investigation will turn up so much, he's finished for sure."

"I don't believe it. I thought rotten guys like that lasted forever."

"Justice prevails now and then."

"Tell me what happened. Tell me all about it."

Angie tossed the carrot into the sink, dried her hands, and eagerly pulled Peter into the living room and onto the couch beside her. "From the very beginning." She squirmed with delight, anticipating the juicy details.

As each new facet emerged, Angie cheered.

"So long, Manny," she intoned when the story ended.

"Sorry we didn't have time to get him a farewell card," Peter added. "The whole department would have loved to sign it." He leaned back with a smug smile. "They're all rejoicing."

"Wow!" Angie exploded. "That's really something." She shook her head slowly, waiting for the facts to sink in. "You mean Manny can't destroy your days anymore?"

"That's right."

"And all the other gardeners are okay to work with, aren't they?"

"Oh, sure."

"Fantastic!" Angie smiled in satisfaction. "Your job should be good now. And you won't always be coming home mad at your partner."

"No."

"Do you know who your new partner will be?"

"Carrie McChesney."

Angie's chin dropped.

"Carrie?" She paused. "A woman?"

"The only woman in the department."

Angie grew thoughtful.

"Is she a real dog?"

"No, she's more of a girl."

"Not old?"

74

"About your age."

Angie was beginning to feel awful inside.

"Is she dirty and sloppy?"

"No, she's nice and clean."

"Oh." Angie's tone was flat. She got up and went back to her carrots.

"Is Carrie McChesney pretty?"

"I'd say she's very nice-looking."

Peter went to clean up. Angie finished preparing dinner.

"How did the second day at Camelot Inn go?" Peter asked as he sat down at the table.

"Mmm, pretty good." There was reservation in Angie's answer.

"Pretty hard work?"

"Not really. The busboys carry the heavy trays. But you have to keep your brains with you."

"Was Luigi pleased with you?"

Angie hesitated. "Him, I'm not so sure about."

Peter waited for more. Angie was silent. When she spoke again, it was with a forced gaiety.

"Well, let's celebrate the end of Manny."

They lifted their coffee mugs in a toast.

"To Manny. May they find him guilty of all the things he's guilty of."

"To Manny."

SEVEN

Peter's mood was mellow as he prepared to leave for work the next day. A day without Manny would be a day full of sunshine, no matter what the weather might be. And working with Carrie, who also loved the park, would be all pleasure.

Peter stopped to kiss Angie good-by. As he did so, he noticed her troubled expression.

"What's the matter, honey?" he asked. "Worried about your new job?"

Angie shook her head.

"What, then?"

"You're going to be sharing your park with another woman."

This took Peter by surprise.

"You're kidding. You're not worried about Carrie?"

"She'll have you all day long, while I'm waiting on tables at Camelot," Angie replied, looking away.

"I'll have Carrie; you'll have Luigi. Fair's fair."

Peter's laughter at his own joke died quickly when he saw Angie's expression as she whirled to confront him.

"Luigi?" he asked tentatively. "Did I say something

wrong? Luigi? Your boss, Luigi?"

"Don't kid about him."

"What's with you? Why are you so touchy?"

"I'm not touchy. I'm fine."

"Yeah, that's why you're wearing that big smile."

"Forget it. Have a good day."

"You, too."

Peter hurried off, not sure what that exchange had been all about.

Carrie was ready and waiting when Peter got to the maintenance yard. She had already checked their assignment and loaded the truck with the proper equipment.

"Do you want to drive, or shall I?" she asked as Peter came out of the office.

"You can," he replied.

With a smile, she slid into the cab.

"You lucky devil," one of the men whispered as Peter opened the other cab door.

"Quit being jealous and think about what I've been through with Manny," Peter whispered back.

What is this? he thought. Everybody seems to think I've got some big thing going because I'm working with a woman. First, Angie. Now, the guys.

Carrie was cheerful and easy to talk to.

"You really like your work, don't you?" Peter commented.

"Yes. It's my first full-time job. I just moved into a place of my own. It's a dump, but it's all mine. And the next thing I'm going to do is get me a little kitten of my own."

"If we'd known, we could have gotten you Fog's sister."

Carried glanced over at Peter. "Fog?"

"That's our kitten."

"Oh." Carrie smiled. "And her sisters are Mist and Rain? The whole damp weather lineup?"

Peter chuckled at her humor.

"My wife, Angie, rescued Fog from the fog in the parking lot of the café where she worked."

"Your wife's an animal lover?"

"Is she ever! All creatures, great and small. She'd adopt them all. But we have this landlord problem. We're not supposed to have pets in our apartment complex."

"So, how do you handle it with Fog?"

"Oh, Fog's a quiet little thing. I don't think anyone knows we have her," Peter replied.

"Manny knows," Carrie said. "I heard him mention once that your wife and her cat were waiting in the car outside the maintenance yard."

"Yeah, Angie puts Fog in a little tote bag and carries her out in the car. She's done it ever since we got Fog. Fog likes riding in—"

Suddenly, Peter stopped talking.

"Oh no," he groaned.

Carrie looked concerned.

"Manny knows we have a cat? Oh no!" Peter sighed. "He could do us in if he wanted to report us."

"And what Manny wants most right now," Carrie replied with an understanding nod, "is to do you in."

Peter closed his eyes and tried not to think about that one. Manny was almost ready to ruin the day, even when he wasn't there.

Back at the apartment, Angie hurried through her last-minute routine before leaving for work. When she picked up Fog for a final hug, she suddenly realized how depressed she was. It was as if a dark storm cloud hovered over her day.

Actually, I should be feeling extra happy instead of down, she told herself. I'm going to a new job, where I want to make good. And Peter's gotten Manny off his back, so he'll come home feeling happy.

"What's my problem?" she asked Fog.

Angie put the kitten down, took her jacket from the closet, and left for work.

I wonder how that Carrie woman is getting along with my husband, Angie worried as she waited for her bus. He'll have nine straight hours, including lunchtime, with that lady gardener. Why couldn't she be old and ugly, Angie wished. Or, better still, be a man.

Angie recalled Peter's joking words. *I'll have Carrie; you'll have Luigi.* Luigi! The thought hit a raw nerve.

Well, let's see how today goes, she cautiously decided. Give it a little time. Maybe I just misunderstood a few things yesterday.

Angie plastered a smile on her face as she got off the bus. Luigi's girls smile, she remembered. A dining room full of dazzling Old English smiles.

She went into the locker room and started changing into her costume. Luigi had scheduled Angie to come in earlier than the other waitresses so he could teach her the job individually. For the moment, she had the whole full-length mirror to herself. She could learn how to adjust her costume to perfection.

Standing in her slip before the mirror, Angie saw the reflection of Luigi in the locker room doorway. To her amazement, he walked right in. Embarrassed, Angie quickly tried to wriggle into her costume.

"Here, let me give you a hand," Luigi said. He hurried over to Angie and helped her slip into the gown.

Instinctively, she drew back as Luigi's hands touched spots they didn't need to touch.

"Honey, don't worry about Papa Luigi," he cooed. "Helping girls is my business."

As Luigi proceeded to adjust the neckline of the gown, his fingers were more inside the lace than was necessary. Angie stepped back and finished the job herself.

"Why are you so skittish about being touched?" Luigi asked.

"I thought I was being trained as a waitress."

"You are, honey. Papa Luigi's training is the very best. Trust me. My girls know how to earn big tips."

"Doing what?" Angie asked suspiciously.

"Just keeping the customers happy."

Luigi reached out to give Angie a pinch on the behind. She stepped back out of reach.

"Don't worry about it," Luigi said in an understanding way. "I'll give you some private instruction after the lunch rush is over. You'll loosen up and be more comfortable. It just takes time, honey."

Angie had a sick feeling inside. What if this job doesn't work out, she thought. My plan! Money to keep Peter in school. I've got to make it work.

The dining room opened, and Angie was plunged into the busy routine. As a trainee, she had been assigned to Maude, one of the other waitresses.

"How long have you worked here?" Angie asked Maude during a lull.

"Eighteen years."

"Has Luigi been here all that time?"

"No. Only the last eight or nine years."

"Can I ask you a funny question, Maude?"

"Sure. Go ahead."

"Is Luigi on the level? I mean does he really train his girls to be waitresses?" Angie was embarrassed. "Do you know what I mean?"

"I know what you mean, Angie, and the answer is that it depends on who you are. Luigi picks out a few girls to give his special training to. His superhostesses, he calls them."

"What do the superhostesses do?"

"Use your imagination, honey. When there's a call for room service, the superhostesses handle the serving . . ."

"And other things." Angie finished Maude's sentence for her. Now her mind was racing.

"Maude, I think Luigi hired me as a trainee for superhostess . . ."

"And . . . ?"

"And that's not what I thought I was being hired for. Somewhere, I read him wrong."

"You sure did, honey. You thought you'd be a regular waitress like me?" Maude laughed. "When old Luigi hires a young one, he has grand plans for her. If he just wants a good waitress, he picks one of us old experienced workhorses."

"Oh, wow!" Angie covered her face with her hands. "He's planning to give me private instruction after lunch. To loosen me up, he says."

"I'll bet!" Maude remarked. "All I can say is you'd better decide before noon what you want, because Luigi is one fast operator."

"Thanks for telling me, Maude."

Angie nervously finished out the shift. All the while, her thoughts were a jumble. She was scared. She didn't know how she would keep Luigi at arm's length.

When the lunch crowd had dwindled, Luigi motioned to Angie to come into his office.

She walked across the dining room and paused at the door. Luigi gestured for her to enter.

"Luigi, I've made a mistake," Angie said, standing at the door.

"Come inside, please."

"But I made a mistake," Angie persisted. "I'm not what you thought you were hiring."

Luigi looked stunned. "Come inside to talk about this, Angie."

Reluctantly she stepped into the office, and Luigi closed the door after her.

Angie hurried on with her explanation. "I didn't know you were hiring me for anything other than a dining room waitress. I was just dumb, I guess. I wanted the job so badly that I didn't pick up your signals."

Luigi was obviously disgusted. "I asked you what made you the right person to train. And you said you'd do anything. I asked you if your husband approved of your applying for this job. And you said he thought anything you wanted to do was okay."

"I just didn't realize—"

"I guess you didn't!" Luigi's tone was cold. "Leave the costume in the locker room."

"I'm sorry, Luigi . . . I . . ."

"Forget it!"

Luigi turned away abruptly and left the room.

Angie tiptoed to the locker room and hastily changed. She hung the costume on a hanger and gave a good-by pat to her dream. Then she hurried out to catch the bus that would take her back to the safety of home.

So much for that plan, Angie sighed wistfully as the Camelot Inn disappeared from view.

The bus trip home seemed endless. From the bus stop, Angie had to force herself every step of the way to the apartment. When she finally closed the apartment door, she leaned against it, her eyes closed, her heart pounding. The tension of the day had left her drained.

How could I possibly have made such a dumb mistake? she kept asking herself, over and over. How? I just wanted a job so badly. I closed my eyes to all the clues, I guess.

Peter. How will I tell him? He'll have spent nine hours with a competent woman who holds down a good job—and then he comes home to a woman who can't even get a lousy job.

Angie picked up Fog and carried her to the bed. She stretched out with the kitten on top of her.

"Why can't I ever seem to get my act together?" she asked Fog. "I don't even know what I want to do . . . I don't know what I want to be . . . Why did I think I wanted the Camelot job when I don't even like being a waitress? . . . I just wanted a job."

Angie dozed off, stroking the kitten and feeling miserable. The ringing of the phone at first seemed like some distant alarm. Then, slowly, Angie pulled herself back to the world. She stumbled over to the phone, trying to get her brain back in focus.

"Hello?"

"Hey, hey, hey, Mrs. Ohlinger. Long time, no see."

Angie froze.

"And what's new with your pussycat?"

Angie couldn't speak.

"I've passed by your apartment complex. Every entrance has a No Pets sign, you know."

Angie nodded silent agreement.

"So I just figure things should be fair. Your husband told my supervisor what he knew about me. I've told your manager what I know about you. That's fair, don't you think?"

Angie furiously shook her head. No!

"Oh, and by the way, keep an eye on your husband's new partner. He got her, you know, because the other married men found her too hot to handle."

Angie felt as if she might throw up.

"Nice talking to you. Hey, hey, Mrs. Ohlinger."

The phone clicked. Angie was holding a dial tone.

EIGHT

PETER had just finished a glorious day. No Manny
. . . a pleasant new partner . . . a park that was really
taking shape. And now, to come home to his wife.
Peter's world was in order.

He sailed into the apartment, ready for a smiling
Angie, who would throw herself into his arms. He
would lift her off her feet and swing her around, laughing. They would drop together onto the bed and talk
over the events of the day. This was homecoming on
the day after Manny. A day to celebrate.

"Angie," Peter called as he opened the door of the
apartment. "Honey, are you home?"

Peter found Angie in a trancelike state, sitting cross-
legged on the bed, like a statue of a woman holding a
cat. He was instantly alarmed.

"Angie?" Peter sat down on the edge of the bed.
"What is it?" He lifted Fog from Angie's arms. The
arms stayed rigid, as if holding a permanent place for
a cat. Peter gently dropped Fog back.

When he waved a hand in front of Angie's eyes,
Peter was relieved to see her begin to come alive. She
turned her head slowly till their eyes met briefly. Then

she buried her tear-streaked face in Fog's fur.

"He knows," she mumbled.

"Who knows what?" Peter was mystified.

"The landlord. He knows we have Fog."

"Mr. Rottweiler? How could he know? Was he here?"

"No. Manny told him."

"Manny what? Manny told the landlord we have a cat?"

"You told on Manny, so he told on you. Fair's fair, he says."

"Where did you hear all this, Angie?"

"From Manny. He phoned."

"You're sure it was Manny? You talked to him?"

"I didn't talk to him. I listened to him. I didn't say anything."

"You're sure it wasn't some joke?"

"Manny's no joke. Yes, I'm sure. Could I ever mistake Manny's 'Hey, hey, hey, Mrs. Ohlinger; what's new, pussycat?' "

Angie ran a hand across her damp cheeks. Peter reached for a tissue for her. Neither spoke.

After a while Peter put his hand on the kitten's head and scratched her ears. Fog purred loudly.

"We can't give her up," he said softly. "Fog is our sunshine."

Angie looked at Peter and broke into tears. "I thought you'd say, 'I told you so.' "

Peter put an arm around Angie. "I told you so," he whispered, "but that's no help now." He shook his head in disbelief. "Who but Manny Schultz would go after a little kitten?"

"What'll we do, Peter?"

"We'll have to think."

Peter gave Angie a teasing poke. "Come on, lady. Let's go get some dinner. We'll think better when we're fed."

Angie began to feel better as they fixed dinner together.

"What else did Manny say?" Peter asked as he set the salads on the table.

Angie gulped, remembering Manny's remark about Carrie. She wondered if her expression would reveal the fact that she knew more than she was telling.

"That was about it," she replied.

"That was plenty."

Angie wanted to change the subject. "How was your day?" she asked when they were seated comfortably at the table.

"Great. They figure three more weeks will finish the park."

"And how was your new partner?" Angie tried to make the question sound casual.

"Very easy to get along with, and a good worker." Peter passed over the question lightly. "How was your day, honey?"

Angie threw her hands up in a gesture of total defeat. "I blew it completely this time, Peter. Do you know what Luigi hired me for?"

"I did wonder about that guy."

"Well, listen to this . . ."

As Angie filled Peter in on the details of her day, he tried to keep a straight face. His response at the end was gentle.

"You learned some things about the big world, huh?"

"Yeah. Talk about getting older and wiser. I left Camelot feeling awful. Then I came home to Manny's phone call, and that was even worse. What will we do, Peter?"

"We could fix up a bassinet and pull the blankets over Fog. Mr. Rottweiler might think we have a new baby," Peter suggested.

Angie couldn't stop laughing.

"Or we could put a big ribbon and a Happy Birthday card around Fog's neck, and stop by to let Mr. Rottweiler admire the gift we're giving to Aunt Dorothy," Peter offered.

Angie loved that one.

Fog, throughout the conversation, remained unworried. As far as she was concerned, she was there to stay. In fact, when Angie and Peter crawled into bed that night, they found that Fog had staked her claim on the foot of the bed.

"Are you sure you're perfectly comfortable?" Peter asked the cat. "Just ring if you want room service. We have a superhostess in this establishment who knows how to keep the guests perfectly happy."

Angie gave her husband a kick.

"Don't call her too soon, though," Peter advised the cat. "She's with another guest at the moment."

The next few days were bad ones. After the Camelot episode, Angie wasn't ready to face any more job interviews for a while. This left her with time on her hands —time to worry, time to brood.

Her plan to get Peter into school was temporarily shelved, without Peter ever knowing the dream had existed. As soon as I can figure out what kind of work I can do, I'll get back to it, she told herself. But I have other things to worry about right now.

She found herself on a downward spiral. Every day

got worse. Peter was worried by the dramatic change in his wife. Grouchy in the mornings, depressed in the evenings, and who knows what in between, he thought.

"Don't you have a girlfriend you could get together with?" he suggested. "Visit, or go shopping, or something. You can't be the only young wife around."

"I don't really have any girlfriends," Angie replied without interest. "In school I spent all my time with you. And I haven't met anyone since."

Why doesn't he just let me dig my hole and crawl in? Angie thought. It will all be over, anyhow, when Mr. Rottweiler comes to evict us for having a cat.

When she wasn't worrying about the landlord, Angie was building a mountain of resentment against Carrie: That woman is only in that work because there are a lot of men around. That woman doesn't worry about whether a guy is married or not. If he's a man, she goes after him. That woman . . . that woman . . . that woman. It burned in Angie's mind like a constant flame.

Manny Schultz's plan was working beyond his wildest dreams. He phoned Angie every day. Shall I answer it? Angie would wonder. When the phone kept ringing, she would end up taking it off the hook. Then she would listen silently, morbidly fascinated, unable to hang up.

Each time the message was the same, with minor variations.

"Hey, hey, hey, Mrs. Ohlinger, keep an eye on your husband's partner. Those lunch hours are getting cozy."

Or, "Notice how happy your husband is when he comes home from work these days."

Or, "You know that grove of trees way back in the

sheltered corner of the park? Well . . ."

And then Angie had the whole day to think about these things—alone. She didn't want to confront Peter with the accusations.

Peter was baffled by his wife's bitterness toward the young woman he worked with. Angie had no reason to doubt his love for her, and yet, she persisted in making cutting remarks and insulting little digs about Carrie.

Peter could only answer, "But she's a nice girl, Angie. She's a lot like you, really. You'd like her if you knew her."

"I can do without that, thanks," Angie would reply curtly.

With that, they would retreat into uncomfortable silence.

During one of the silent evenings, the doorbell rang. Angie tensed. She clutched Fog.

"It's got to be Mr. Rottweiler," she whispered. "I can't face it. You handle it, Peter."

Angie tiptoed into the bedroom with Fog in her arms. Peter waited till she closed the door, and then strode toward the front door. He took a deep breath, let it out in a soft sigh, then opened the door a crack. It was Mr. Rottweiler.

"Good evening, Peter."

The landlord's old European air of dignity made Peter respond with formality.

"How do you do, Mr. Rottweiler." He opened the door wide for the landlord. "Come in, please."

"Thank you. I can only stay a moment."

Peter offered the older man a chair, but remained standing himself.

"I'm really sorry about it, sir," Peter began hastily explaining. "She'll be gone very soon." He paced nervously as he spoke. "She can stay with my sister until other arrangements can be made."

Mr. Rottweiler looked stricken. "Oh, my boy, that's very sad!"

"Yeah, we're pretty torn up about it."

"But, of course you are."

"From the beginning we were afraid it could never work. But you know how it is . . ."

"I do, my boy, I certainly do."

"When you go into these things, there's always the hope that everything will work out. And then it's so awful to have to give up the dream. I don't know how we'll say good-by."

Mr. Rottweiler's eyes filled with tears. "I know you love her terribly."

"Yeah, she's brought so much sunshine."

Mr. Rottweiler nodded sympathetically as Peter continued.

"And to have it all ended by a rotten guy like Manny Schultz. Just one poison phone call, and . . . and it's all over."

"Oh, you poor boy. Another man. That lovely wife of yours, to leave you for another man!"

"Huh?"

"Your marriage breaking up."

"What? Oh no, Mr. Rottweiler!"

"But you just said . . . didn't you just say it's all over because of this man?"

Peter suddenly went limp. He dropped into a chair.

"Didn't Manny Schultz phone you, saying we had a cat?"

"Oh, that," Mr. Rottweiler scoffed. "I did receive an anonymous phone call from some man, saying there was a cat in this apartment. But that wasn't news to me.

I saw the kitten several days ago when I checked smoke alarms."

"Why didn't you say something then, Mr. Rottweiler?"

"With all the big problems we have in this apartment complex, one little cat doesn't worry me, my boy. The only pets I evict are the ones that disturb other tenants or destroy my property. If no one ever complains about your cat, then she's of no concern to me."

"You mean you didn't come to tell us to get rid of the cat or we'd be evicted?" Peter asked incredulously.

"Not at all." Mr. Rottweiler shook his head, bewildered by the turn the conversation had taken. "And you weren't telling me your wife was leaving?"

"Not at all. I was saying we were making plans for Fog if we couldn't keep her here." Peter jumped up. "I've got to tell Angie. Okay? Don't go away, Mr. Rottweiler."

Peter opened the bedroom door. Angie, all smiles, had obviously been listening through the door. She rushed toward Mr. Rottweiler, holding Fog in her arms.

"You're an absolute doll, Mr. Rottweiler."

Peter shot Angie a cautioning glance.

"I mean you're a wonderful gentleman. Thank you. Thank you very much."

Mr. Rottweiler beamed, embarrassed.

"Would you like a cup of tea?" Angie asked.

"Thank you, my dear. That would be very nice." He turned to Peter. "Now, what I really came for was to ask you a favor."

"Of course. What can I do for you?"

"I know you are a gardener for the city. I wondered if you might know some gardener who would want to take on the grounds of this apartment complex as an after-hours job. 'Moonlighting,' I think it's called here. I'd give free rent in one of our garden apartments in exchange for the services."

"H'mm," Peter said, obviously deep in thought.

Angie watched Peter slowly beginning to light up. They had never discussed her dream of helping him go to college, yet from the look on Peter's face, it was clear he had been cherishing a dream of his own.

"I'll take it, Mr. Rottweiler. I'll take it myself. In fact, it might be a perfect answer." Peter was glowing. "I've wanted to get into Crestline's program—and this may be the way I can do it."

Angie's emotions were on a seesaw, going up and down, up and down. Her relief about Fog was enormous, and seeing Peter suddenly come alive with plans was just what she had wanted. But—and that was where Angie's nerves were raw—but these new plans would be successful only if she were working at a steady job.

Torn two ways, smiling and shaking, Angie served Mr. Rottweiler his tea and cookies.

"You're such a lovely wife, my dear. It was very unnerving to think of you and Peter breaking up."

"*You* were unnerved!" Angie blurted out. "Think how *I* felt, hiding behind a door, hearing my husband say, 'She'll be gone very soon. From the beginning we were afraid it could never work.' "

Peter, uneasy about Angie's candor, watched for a reaction from the older man.

Mr. Rottweiler leaned over to speak confidentially to Peter, man to man. "I think the lady deserves a cat," he said softly. "She's earned it."

Peter closed the door after Mr. Rottweiler left and leaned against it, grinning.

"Well, old Manny lost the war!" he gloated. "Fog's a legitimate Ohlinger now, you might say."

"Super," Angie sighed. "She can come out of the closet."

Peter picked up the kitten and looked into her eyes. "Was it tough being a closet cat?" he asked.

Angie appeared amused, but deep down she was not laughing. Peter could go ahead and celebrate the end of the war if he wanted to, but she knew the war was only half over.

Peter put the cat down and grew serious.

"Well, what do you think?" he asked Angie.

"About the new job, you mean? Well, it'll be hard to handle along with your city job."

"I can do it on weekends," Peter said. "I figure if I begin the job now and Mr. Rottweiler starts paying our rent, we can put our rent money away each month until school starts in September. Then when I quit work and start classes, we'll have a little in the bank to tide us over."

"In case I still don't have a job!" Angie felt touchy about that subject.

"Something like that."

Peter looked Angie squarely in the eye. "Do you want me to do it, or not? If you don't, I'll forget the whole thing."

What do I tell him? Angie wondered. That I'm such a mess I don't know if anyone will hire me by September? That I can't even think of a job I could do well? That I'm finished with school without even knowing what I can be?

Angie looked away, not daring to meet Peter's gaze. "Yes, I want you to do it," she said haltingly. "I had planned on putting you through school with my tips from the Camelot job. But now . . ." Angie shivered. "Now, I'm scared, Peter."

"What are you scared of?"

Peter sensed that Angie had more trouble than she was admitting. He sat down by her quietly.

"I'm scared that I'm never going to *be* anything."

"You *are* something right now, Angie—you're yourself, and you're my wife."

"But I'm no good for a job. What can I do?"

"You'll find something, honey." Peter patted Angie's hand and got up to carry the dishes to the sink.

"I don't understand it," he said over his shoulder as he rinsed the dishes. "We should be walking on air tonight—celebrating like crazy. Manny lost, we won, Fog's safe with us, we'll get one of the garden apartments, the way is opening for college. All of this, and it's a downer! What on earth is wrong?"

"Everything!" Angie said, walking to the bedroom. She flopped facedown on the bed. Wondering what new suspicions Manny's next phone call would raise, she fell into restless sleep.

The next morning at breakfast, Angie was withdrawn and silent. Peter, tired of gloomy meals, didn't try to make conversation. Instead, he turned his thoughts to his work for the day.

"Oh, by the way," he remarked as he was leaving, "the department is having a barbecue on Saturday at the Hubbard Avenue Park, to celebrate its completion. You'll enjoy it, I think. The wives and kids will all be there, and there'll be a lot of good food."

Angie shrugged her shoulders. Peter left.

That's what I really want, she thought, a chance to see Carrie McChesney in person, drooling over my husband. And, from what Manny says, my husband will be drooling right back.

The thought of appearing at a party chilled Angie. The other wives will have either children or jobs—and some will have both—she worried. What could I possibly say if they ask me what I do? "Oh, I'm staying home waiting for life to begin. No, I don't do anything. I'm not anything." And if I should have to meet Carrie, what would I do? What on earth would I say to her?

The more Angie considered the barbecue, the more she knew it was not what she wanted to do with a Saturday.

What *do* I want to be doing with a Saturday? she wondered. Come to think of it, Saturdays, Sundays, Mondays—they all look alike these days. Just time to be got through.

By afternoon, Angie's thinking was beginning to change. On the other hand, she was saying to herself, maybe, just maybe, I shouldn't let Carrie have Peter without a fight. I think I might go to the barbecue—and if that woman wants Peter Ohlinger, she can take him over the dead body of *Mrs.* Peter Ohlinger.

While Angie was making this decision, the phone rang. Angie let it ring and ring. When it became clear that the caller was not giving up, she finally reached for the instrument. Without speaking, she lifted the receiver.

"Hey, hey, hey, Mrs. Ohlinger. Are you going to move, or will you choose to give up your cat? Have you decided? H'mmmm?"

For the first time, Angie felt compelled to answer Manny's taunts.

"You turkey!" she said, her voice dripping with disgust.

She slammed down the receiver. Standing there, looking angrily at the phone, she felt a sudden surge of new energy.

I will not lie down and play dead, she announced firmly to herself. I'll fight to keep my man! And that little Carrie had better watch out!

NINE

WHEN Peter came home that evening, he was surprised at the change in Angie. She was hardly what he would call soft and cuddly, but at least she acted alive. For the first time since the days of Camelot, there seemed to be a spark of energy in his wife.

To Peter's amazement, Angie brought up the subject of the barbecue. He had already decided he would go alone, rather than urge Angie to join him and then have her stand around at the party like a storm cloud.

"Are we supposed to bring anything to the barbecue?" she asked.

"They put me down for a green salad," Peter answered. "If that's okay with you?"

"Why not," Angie replied, almost agreeably.

She went to the kitchen and started serving the dinner, which was ready for a change. Peter was stunned.

"I think I'll wear my blue outfit with the white turtleneck," Angie said in an offhand way.

"Great. You look good in it!" Peter was enthusiastic.

I'll show that little Carrie a thing or two, Angie promised herself.

"Our job at the park is all done," Peter remarked over dinner.

"Yours and Carrie's, you mean?"

"I mean the planting is finished."

"What's next?"

"The other crews have to put the final touches on the picnic area and the children's playground. The ball park and rest rooms are completed."

"I meant what's next for you?"

"I don't know. I'll have to wait for a new assignment."

"Will Carrie still be your work partner?"

"I don't know that, either. I hope so. She's the best partner I've ever had."

Wonderful, Angie thought.

They lapsed into silence. Lately, they had almost gotten used to listening to the clink of their silverware and the sounds of their chewing.

Finally Angie spoke. "Manny phoned."

"He did?" Peter was alarmed. "What did he say?"

"He wanted to know if we were going to move or give up our cat instead?"

"Surprise for Manny! What did you tell him?"

Angie felt a tingle of excitement, just recalling the incident. She had to hold back a grin as she told about it.

"I just said, 'You turkey!' and hung up."

"All right! Beautiful, Angie. I knew you had it in you."

Angie ducked her head, embarrassed but pleased.

"I'm so proud of you. It couldn't have been stated more perfectly. What a classic end for Manny!"

I wish, Angie thought.

When the day of the barbecue arrived, Peter would rather have been anywhere else. During the final days preceding the event, Angie had been so high-strung and nervous that conversation was impossible. She frequently asked Peter about Carrie, and then made barbed comments about his answers. Peter, nevertheless, kept hoping the day could be saved.

"You look nice," he said reassuringly as Angie climbed into the car to go to the park.

"Thanks," she replied stiffly. Her smile was frozen, her body tense.

Most of the crowd was already there when Peter and Angie arrived at the picnic. The meat was barbecuing and the tables were set. Groups were forming, seats were being saved.

Angie noticed Peter breaking into a smile. Glancing over her shoulder, she saw a young woman approaching.

"Angie, this is Carrie," Peter said.

This was the moment the world was supposed to stop for Angie. She had rehearsed it so many times in her mind that she could play the scene backward, and now it was moving so fast that she wasn't even ready with her lines.

"Why don't you sit with us, Carrie?" Peter suggested.

"Okay, thanks," Carrie replied.

Peter led the two women to a table and sat down between them. If Angie wanted to play her scene, she was going to have to shout her lines across her husband.

Angie kept stealing furtive looks at Carrie, trying to

get used to what she was seeing. Carrie wasn't what she'd expected—not at all.

She's certainly not the red-hot number Manny said she was, Angie had to concede grudgingly. Her whole scene was going to lose its punch if Carrie wasn't a sexpot.

Actually, she doesn't look any better than I do, Angie decided, much to her own surprise. And she's not hanging all over my husband. She's talking to the woman on the other side of her more than to Peter.

She's not grubby, either, was Angie's final concession. Her fingernails and hands are clean, and she's wearing a nice opal ring.

Well, at least I don't have to talk to her, Angie thought. I can't imagine what we would ever have in common to talk about. Thank goodness Peter's between us.

In a matter of minutes, Carrie the Threat had dwindled to Carrie the Bore. This permitted Angie to be civil at lunch, if nothing more.

All during the meal, Angie's mind was churning. It just doesn't fit, she kept saying to herself—all those awful things Manny was saying on the phone about Carrie, and look at her. She's just a girl, not gorgeous, not ugly, not slinky-sexy—just somewhere in between, like most of us.

Angie's hostility was shifting to a different target. What a crummy excuse for a man, that Manny Schultz! That's a rotten thing to do to a girl like Carrie—to pass out awful lies about her, to get her partner's wife jealous enough really to go after her. Poor kid, she has no idea what Manny's been doing to her. She doesn't even know how much I've been hating her, or why.

Angie hardly touched her lunch. She had been too busy thinking.

"You okay, honey?" Peter asked.

"Just not very hungry," Angie replied.

"Anybody for softball?" one of the men called. "Peter? Come on, join us. Does your wife play?"

Angie shook her head vigorously.

"Carrie?"

Carrie shook her head, too.

"Do you mind if I play for a little while?" Peter asked Angie.

"I'll be okay," she told him. "Go ahead and play."

Peter and the other softball players moved over to the ball park. Angie and Carrie were left sitting at the picnic table, with an empty space between them.

They glanced uncertainly at each other, and then Carrie slid closer to Angie.

"Can I get some advice from you, Angie?" Carrie asked shyly.

"Sure, Carrie." Angie was taken by surprise.

"Peter says you're great with animals, and you know everything about pets."

Angie smiled to think Peter had been talking about her to Carrie.

"I want to get a cat, and I don't know how to find one that will be just right for me."

"Oh, you'd love one like Fog," Angie said.

"Peter told me about Fog. She sounds adorable—the way you carry her around in a tote bag and everything."

"If you want a cat, Carrie, you want a Fog. Believe me."

Just thinking of the kitten made Angie smile. "Hey," she said on a sudden impulse. "Do you want to go see

Fog while they play softball?"

"Yeah, I'd love to."

"Oh, darn, I don't have the car keys," Angie said.

"I have my car. Let's go," Carrie urged. "I'm parked out back. I work here, so I know the shortcuts."

"Do you like being a gardener?" Angie asked as they wove through the traffic.

"I really do. And the guys have been so decent to me. Since I'm the only woman gardener, I expected a lot of resentment and raunchy jokes. But out of the entire crew, only one guy ever tried to get fresh."

"Peter Ohlinger, I suppose?" Angie said with a teasing little grin.

They both giggled.

"Only kidding, of course," Angie hastily added.

"No, it was a guy named Manny Schultz. Ever hear of him from Peter?"

"Worse! I've heard of him from *him!* Let me tell you about Manny Schultz and Fog."

Carrie listened intently to the trials of Fog. At the end, she said, "Manny's such a jerk. I'm surprised he didn't try to get back at me, too, for rejecting his propositions. He could have made up a lot of lies to turn the guys, and even their wives, against me."

Angie's weeks of resentment and anger were still vivid in her mind. Carrie just didn't know how bad Manny's attacks on her had been.

Angie took a deep breath before she answered. She needed time to think. Her answer to Carrie had to be worded very carefully.

"You're lucky, Carrie. You don't seem to be one of Manny's victims." Angie smiled at Carrie, and Carrie grinned back.

"Thank goodness he didn't go after me," Carrie said

with a sigh, "or you and I might never have become friends."

"Oh, I almost forgot—turn left at the next intersection," Angie said. "We're the first building on the right just beyond the corner."

Carrie pulled into a parking space. "Now," she said, "to meet the kitten who survived Manny Schultz."

"I think," Angie added, almost in a whisper, "that you're talking to a woman who survived him, too."

Carrie raised a questioning eyebrow.

"I'll tell you the story some other time," Angie said.

As Angie opened the apartment door, Fog lifted her head above the side of her box, her mouth spread wide in a yawn. Angie picked up the kitten so Carrie could look into the furry face.

"And this is our sunshine named Fog," she said.

"Oh, she is a sunbeam," Carrie murmured, reaching for the cat. Fog snuggled into her arms and started to purr. "I've been so anxious to get my own place so I could have my own cat."

"Do you have your own apartment now?"

"It's not an apartment; it's a dump. But I was lucky to get it. I'd love to find something like this someday." Carrie's eyes were moving around the room. "You really know how to make a place cute, Angie."

"You like it? Our style is called Early Cheap."

"I love it. I wish I had your knack. I have a great kitchen herb garden, but I haven't figured out yet what to do with the rest of the apartment."

"Do you know how to cook with herbs?" Angie asked, impressed.

"I'm learning," Carrie replied. "I saw an announcement about an adult school class in herb cooking, but

I haven't taken it, because I'm kind of chicken about going to night school alone."

"Hey, maybe we could go together. Peter has been saying he wants an herb garden, and I've been saying I wouldn't know what to do with herbs if he grew them."

"Great. Let's do it."

"Okay."

Angie went to the refrigerator and poured a couple of sodas. She motioned for Carrie to sit down. Carrie, still holding Fog, chose the rocking chair.

"Do you work, Angie?"

Angie's heart stopped. Carrie had asked that awful question. How do you tell a woman with a good job that you don't even know where to look for a job you could handle?

Carrie was holding Fog's face close to hers, rubbing noses.

Angie took a chance. "Let me tell you about my last job. I had it for three days. There was this guy named Luigi . . ."

By the time Angie had finished the story about Luigi's superhostesses, both girls were in stitches. Carrie couldn't stop laughing. She'd think of some part of the story and start in again.

"That's my career," Angie said.

When Carrie finally stopped laughing, she was quiet for a moment. "So what are you going to try next?" she asked.

"I've been afraid to even think about that. I'm just not right for a lot of jobs. I guess I belong in the zoo, cleaning animal cages. I get along great with animals."

"Hey . . ." Carrie started to speak and then paused,

trying to remember something. "I saw an article about the SPCA's Animal Grooming School. It trains people to be professional animal groomers."

Angie tensed with excitement. "Grooming animals? As a career? To make money?"

"I guess so. I don't know much about it, but I think I know where the article is."

"Learn to groom animals . . ." Angie's mind was working furiously. "Now that sounds more like me. I could be really good at that."

"Better than superhostessing for Luigi?" Carrie giggled.

"Could you find me the details, Carrie?"

"I'll phone you tonight about them."

Angie looked at the clock. "We'd better get back. The ball game probably is about over."

Carrie was still hugging Fog.

"We'll have to find you a Fog of your own, Carrie." Angie's mind raced ahead. "Maybe I might even find you one at the grooming school."

"Good. Keep your eyes open for me."

Carrie wrote down Angie's phone number, then set Fog down in her box.

"It was really nice coming here, Angie." Carrie was reluctant to leave. "Working with only men, I get lonely for a girlfriend."

"Me too," Angie confessed. "I only see my husband."

As they drove back to the park, Angie glanced over at Carrie. "Would you believe that I've been hating you for weeks, Carrie? You were with my husband nine hours every day, and I was sure you were taking him away from me."

Carrie looked surprised. "You're kidding. Take Peter

away from you? That's a joke. He talks about you all the time. You and Fog. You two must have something going that the rest of us can only envy."

"Uh-huh," Angie agreed softly. "We do . . . if I can give it a little boost to get it back into shape."

TEN

THE ball game was still going on when Angie and Carrie parked behind the picnic area and slipped back in. Peter was no longer in the softball game. He was pacing nervously around the park, looking for the two women.

He had only joined the ball game in order to give Angie and Carrie a few minutes together. His plan was to get replaced early in the game and return right away to be with the women, acting as a referee, or peace-maker, or whatever was needed to keep them from clawing each other to pieces.

Peter had left the softball game ten minutes after it started and hurried back to the picnic area. The two women were gone. Nobody seemed to know anything about them, no traces were left behind. Instant com-bustion, Peter thought grimly, but no little pile of ashes.

Considering Angie's hostility toward Carrie and her recent mood swings, Peter wasn't just uneasy, he was worried. I never should have left them alone together, he chided himself. I should have stayed between them. If it was too much for them to handle, it's my fault. He nervously twisted a stalk of grass and kept looking.

Angie and Carrie spotted Peter from a distance and waved to him. Peter, startled, did a double take. He must be seeing wrong—it had to be two other young women, not Angie and Carrie. These women were smiling and laughing, their heads together, their pace lively. He was looking for a bedraggled pair who had fought it out one way or another—survivors.

"Hey," Angie yelled, "what's the matter? Don't you wave at beautiful women?"

Peter blinked. The two women grinned and approached him.

"Looking for someone?" Angie asked as she sidled up close.

"Oh, I was looking for my gloomy wife and my grumpy partner. But you two look better. Why don't I forget about them and take up with you two instead?"

"Good idea," Carrie told him.

"Where were you?" Peter asked Angie. "I've been looking all over for you."

"We thought you would be playing softball for a while," Angie replied. "We went to our place. Carrie wanted to see Fog. Oh, and you know that herb garden you wanted to plant? Well, why don't you start it? Carrie and I are going to take a class in herb cooking."

"Whew!" Peter said.

Carrie looked at her watch. "I'm going to get going now, but I'll phone you tonight, Angie."

"Thanks, Carrie. Bye."

Peter watched this exchange, dumbfounded.

"What's the matter?" Angie asked.

"Uh . . ." Peter had to readjust his thinking. He had been prepared for a lot of things; he had anticipated every kind of problem. But, friendship? That one he had not figured on. "Uh . . . well . . . well . . . I was just wondering if you'd like to walk around the park, maybe, and see what I planted."

"Well . . ." Angie hesitated.

"That's okay," Peter hastily replied. "Forget it if you don't want to." He didn't want his trees dragged into any family conflict.

"Well, really," Angie said, "I just think it would be better if we looked at what you *and* Carrie planted. A team is a team, after all, and she should get some credit."

"Come on, lady!" Peter grabbed Angie's hand. "Let me show you the park. Just let me. . . . There happens to be a nice secluded corner way over there . . ."

He winked at Angie. "A little grassy spot, surrounded by *Dendrocalamus latifolius.*"

"Oh, *Dendrocalamus latifolius,*" Angie said, nodding wisely. "They're the best."

That evening Angie hovered near the phone. When it finally rang, she caught it on the first ring. Then it occurred to her that all her phone calls lately had been from Manny, and she had always waited till the fifteenth ring before answering.

"Hi," she said, certain it would be Carrie.

"Hi, Angie."

"It's sure nice to pick up a phone and not hear 'Hey, hey, hey, Mrs. Ohlinger.' "

Carrie groaned. "Manny's greeting, of course. Has he called you a lot?"

"Well, some." Angie's reply was cautious. "About Fog and the landlord, you know. I told you about it."

"Yeah. Well, I found the article about the Animal Grooming School for you. There's a phone number and an address where you can get more information. Got a pencil?"

"All ready." Angie jotted down the information.

"Let me know what you find out."

"Oh, sure. Thanks a lot, Carrie."

"Say hello to Peter."

"Okay. Bye."

Smiling, Angie hung up the phone. She folded the paper and slipped it into her purse.

"What was that?" Peter asked, curious because Angie's answers had revealed so little.

"It was Carrie. She said hello to you."

"That was all?"

"More or less."

"What was that part about Manny?"

"Well, you know," Angie said evasively.

"No, I don't know. Tell me! How many times has Manny called you? Angie!" Peter's tone was firm.

"Quite a few."

"How many is quite a few?"

"A whole lot. Like every weekday for the last couple of weeks." Angie's voice faded out.

Peter started pacing around the room. "Why didn't you tell me?" he asked.

"It was too awful, and I started believing it—it was all this stuff about you and Carrie."

Peter looked stunned.

"Stuff about me and Carrie? You mean Manny was phoning every day and telling you things about Carrie and me?"

Peter sat down on the edge of the couch, staring between his knees at the floor.

"And you began to believe those things?" His voice was almost a whisper.

"I didn't want to."

"But it was hard not to?"

Angie nodded solemnly.

Peter shook his head slowly. "I didn't know. I had no idea. So that's why you hated Carrie!"

Angie nodded again.

"Did you really think I had something going with Carrie?"

"I was afraid you might."

Peter motioned for Angie to come to him and sit on his lap. He put his arms around her.

"Honey, next time—if there should ever be a next time—why don't you tell me what you've heard before you believe it. I'd like to give you the facts straight, if the story involves me."

"That might work better," Angie agreed.

Peter still couldn't get used to the idea. "You really believed I'd be messing around with another woman?"

"I don't now. Not after what Carrie told me about you."

Peter perked up. "Oh? What did Carrie say about me?"

"Never mind. It was girl talk."

"What was the rest of Carrie's phone message? What you wrote down and put in your purse?"

"More girl talk."

Peter knew he wasn't going to get any more out of Angie on that subject.

"That's what you get for marrying a woman," Angie told him as she kissed him. "You get women."

"Yeah," Peter agreed. "They're the best kind."

On Monday morning Peter looked closely at his wife, as she sat opposite him eating breakfast.

"You look different, honey, excited. You have kind of a glow."

"Do I?" Angie tried to sound innocent.

"Come on, what's doing?" Peter hoped to tease a little information out of Angie.

"I'll tell you tonight."

Peter suddenly dropped his fork on the plate. "Hey . . . all this woman talk with Carrie. Are you by any chance going to the doctor today? Angie, do you think you might be pregnant?"

Angie looked at Peter's earnest expression. "No, I'll at least put your mind to rest on that. Today has nothing to do with a baby." Angie raised her right hand. "I swear. But it may have something to do with you and me and our future."

"Want to pass out any other clues?"

"Nope. Tonight."

Peter resigned himself to waiting until evening. With a kiss for Angie, he left for work.

Angie left almost immediately to check out the Animal Grooming School.

The minute she entered the SPCA building, Angie knew she was in tune with the organization. She felt at home with the atmosphere and the people. And the grooming school seemed tailor-made for her talents and needs. Angie moved through her day of discovery with high enthusiasm.

Once during the day, she stopped short to caution herself. It seems too good to be true, she thought. And so did Camelot Inn, at first.

No, this is different, she concluded. Totally different. Now I'm in the right place. These are my kind of people. Angie could hardly wait for evening, when she could share it all with Peter.

The time finally came. Peter dropped onto the couch. "Okay! Now it's tonight," he pointed out. "It's kiss-and-tell time. Tell first; then kiss."

"All right. Here it is. I'm on the waiting list to go to school!"

"School? But you've always said . . ."

"This one is my kind of school. There are four students in the class, and the teachers are all animals. All, that is, except one human instructor."

"You're right, that sounds like your style of classroom."

"Peter," Angie said with obvious pride, "I'm going to become a professional animal groomer."

"A professional animal groomer?" Peter wasn't expecting that. "What do you know?" he said admiringly. "You've hit something that sounds like *you*. Where is this school?"

"It's at the SPCA. I'll go to school for three months, forty hours a week. Then, when I get my diploma, I'll be ready for a real job, earning money, just in time for you to start your fall semester at Crestline."

"Are there jobs?" Peter asked.

"So far, they've placed every graduate in a good position. I can be a groomer for a shop, or I could groom show animals. And someday I might even set up my own business."

Angie looked at Peter proudly. "So, I'll go to school first, and then you can take your turn. But—smart me, I'll graduate in three months, and you'll take years."

Peter put his arms around Angie. "I can just see you there, with your sleeves rolled up, loading those dogs into the washers and dryers. This guy gets five minutes on regular cycle, heavy-duty detergent, lots of bleach. This one, give her delicate cycle, just a little Ivory

Snow, a bit of softener. That guy, uh-oh, he says dry clean only."

Angie grinned and hugged her husband.

Peter went on. "Will I have to sign the deficiency notices that the school sends home? 'Your wife gave Lassie a full haircut, when all she wanted was a shampoo. Your wife put the poodle in the hot dry, and he ended up with the frizzies.' "

Angie laughed.

"And what about your report cards?" Peter wanted to know. "Will you be graded with woofs, arfs, and grrrs?"

"Never mind," Angie replied. "When I graduate with honors, my diploma, signed with the dean's paw print, will look pretty fancy hanging next to your plain old diploma from Crestline College."

Peter pulled himself loose from Angie's hug and headed for the kitchen drawer. He returned with a hammer and a nail.

Studying the wall to find just the right position, he pounded in the nail. Then he picked up Fog and stepped back a few feet to view the position of the nail critically.

"That," he said to the cat, "is for your mother's diploma. 'Angela Curry Ohlinger' it will say."

"How about that!" Angie said with a touch of awe in her voice. She went over to the wall and made an imaginary adjustment in the angle of her imaginary diploma.

Then she went to the kitchen for another nail. Measuring carefully, Angie pounded her nail into the wall near Peter's, then looked at him with a triumphant smile.

"Let's make it a his-and-hers set."

Purring loudly, Fog nuzzled Peter's ear. Peter held very still, listening to the cat.

"No," he whispered into the furry ear, "that's okay —you don't have to get a diploma to stay in the family. You can just stick around and teach your mother about cats."

Peter watched Angie's expression. "And I'll just—" he winked at Angie, "just stick around."

About the Author

PHYLLIS ANDERSON WOOD teaches basic reading
and writing skills at Westmoor High School in Daly
City, near San Francisco. The reactions of her own students strongly influence her writing. A graduate of the
University of California at Berkeley, she completed a
graduate year in drama and education at Stanford University, and holds an M.A. from San Francisco State
University.